KING'S EX

ROYAL
POWERS

E.J. Russell

Cover art: Fern Lee
Edited by Meg DesCamp

ISBN: 978-1-947033-26-9

First edition
February, 2021

Contact information:
ejr@ejrussell.com

KING'S EX

ROYAL
POWERS

E.J. Russell

The world of Royal Powers is not so different from our own.
Except for the two mythical countries on the France/Spain border.
And the two extra royal families.
Oh, and that superpowers thing.
But otherwise, you know, pretty much the same.

CHAPTER ONE

"Gaston, you're pulling your punches again." Bastien easily parried his guard captain's strike and reversed his own staff to tap Gaston's chest over his protective vest.

"Call it an excess of caution, Your Majesty." Gaston retreated two paces and bowed, acknowledging the touch. "I don't want to be tossed in the dungeons for hitting the king."

"We're sparring. Not engaged in mortal combat." Bas planted his staff on the mat at his feet. "How am I to learn if you don't give me your best?"

Gaston lifted his helmet's face shield. "You've learned plenty, Your Majesty." He wiped the sweat off his forehead with the back of his hand. "Give me a workout, you do."

"'Plenty' isn't exactly my aim." Bas removed his own helmet. Although he'd been exerting himself nearly as much as Gaston, he, of course, hadn't broken a sweat.

He never did.

"Be that as it may, Your Majesty, you'll do." He grinned as he stripped off his vest. "Same time next Monday?"

"Sooner, I think." Bas unbuckled his own protective vest and slipped it off. It was as pristine as when he'd donned it forty-five minutes ago, his bare chest underneath also devoid of perspiration. "With Bonfire Fortnight kicking off today, my governmental obligations are significantly reduced." And Bas needed the release of physical activity to get him through the damned festivities. "Let us say Friday at the usual time?"

Gaston bowed, one fist over his heart. "Of course, Your Majesty."

"And Gaston?" His captain of the guards lifted an inquiring eyebrow. "Be sure to take some time off for yourself over the next fortnight as well."

Gaston chuckled. "Not likely, Your Majesty. Where you go, we go."

"Just as well I won't be going anywhere until after the fireworks next week, then, isn't it?"

Gaston shrugged as he placed his quarterstaff in the rack on the private gym's wall. "The New Palace can be just as dangerous as the streets, Majesty." He grinned at Bas over his shoulder. "Especially with all those extra Royals in residence for the celebrations."

Bas groaned. "Don't remind me."

Bonfire Fortnight was all the excuse North Abarran Royals of any degree needed to descend on the New Palace and strain the Chamberlain's staff to the limit. Add the fact that Bas's birthday fell midway through the holidays—and that this year marked his thirty-third, a traditional milestone for North Abarran kings—and the next two weeks promised to be a madhouse.

"Promise to protect me from everyone who's intent on pressing unnecessary birthday gifts on me in hopes of later political favor?"

Gaston pulled a plain gray sweatshirt over his head. "The guards'll collect the gifts as usual, Your Majesty. The political favors? Those are up to you."

Bas sighed, perhaps a bit over-dramatically. "Sadly, I fear you are correct." He inclined his head. "Until your next shift, then."

Gaston clicked his heels together, which oddly wasn't any less crisp and impressive when he was barefoot than when he was wearing his uniform boots. He marched out of the room as Bas wandered over to stow his own quarterstaff.

"What the fuck are you wearing?"

Bas's smile broke out at the sound of his cousin's voice, the irascible tone as familiar to him as his own hand. He turned unhurriedly to face Tarik Jaso, Duke of Arles and prince of the blood. "Tarik," he drawled. "What a pleasant surprise."

Tarik snorted. "Right. Don't evade the question."

Bas held his arms out, putting himself on display, and glanced down at his body. "I assume you're referring to my Landsknecht trousers, since from what I understand of the antics you and your husband get up to—and not always in the privacy of your own quarters—you're quite familiar with bare skin."

After Tarik's marriage, his former habitual scowl had been replaced by an almost perpetual grin. It dawned now, his brown cheeks creased in dimples that Bas hadn't known existed. "Don't let envy turn you sour, Bas." He sauntered into the gym. "Has it really caused you to go into such a decline that you've taken to wearing bloomers?"

Bas lifted his chin in faux-haughtiness as he held out the sides of the trousers, the better to reveal the forest green fabric pleated beneath their slashes. "I'll have you know, this is traditional garb for quarterstaff combat."

"Traditional in the Middle Ages," Tarik muttered, although he didn't lose the grin. "Wouldn't modern workout gear be more comfortable?"

"Perhaps." Bas glanced down at the trousers that ballooned over his thighs to the cuffs secured beneath his knees. "But as much as I challenge traditions in other places, I prefer to honor them when I can."

Tarik chuckled. "You mean when it doesn't inconvenience you and you can indulge your penchant for fancy dress."

Bas winced. "Is that the chatter you're picking up these days?" Tarik, with his powers as Wavelength, could pick up messages sent on any frequency. Given the unrest that still roiled over the new detente with South Abarra—exemplified by Tarik's own marriage to a South Abarran duke—Tarik had been monitoring the airwaves relentlessly. "That I'm a vain peacock, only interested in my own convenience and appearance, regardless of what my subjects might be suffering?"

Tarik's smile faded. "Fuck, Bas. That's not what I— I was just taking the mickey out of you, same as always."

"But have you picked up anything?"

Tarik shrugged. "Nothing out of the ordinary. Nothing about Sander and me at all." He plucked a hand weight from a wall rack and absently lifted it in a series of biceps curls. "Seems like everyone is more concerned about getting drunk off their asses for the next two weeks and roasting marshmallows over effigies of our dear, dear ancestor, may he burn in hell."

"Amen to that," Bas murmured as he collected his soft cotton robe. Instead of putting it on, though, he let it hang limp in his hand.

"There's some of the usual grumbling. Complaints about how much better South Abarrans have it than we do with the new trade agreements."

Bas gifted Tarik with a glare. "The reason South Abarrans have it better is because they're not fighting the alliance."

"They seem to be a less contentious lot, it's true." He wrinkled his nose. "Some of my more distant in-laws being the exceptions."

Bas chuckled. "Is Princess Bianca still calling rainstorms down on your head?"

"I've surrendered to the inevitable, but luckily Sander's so pissed at her that he won't let her onto the estate anymore. No. It's Otho. He's finally started to talk."

"Otho?" Bas blinked. "He's naming his co-conspirators at last?" Otho's participation in the kidnapping and attempted murder of Tarik and Sander had landed him in the Dulibre prison, considerably less cushy accommodations than he'd apparently expected, the fool.

Tarik's face twisted in disgust. "If only. No. Somehow he heard the story of what happened at the wedding, and he's claiming he was a victim of mind control. That Mastermind made him do it."

"If Mastermind did as many things as criminals claim he does, he wouldn't have time to take a piss."

"True. But…" Tarik's voice took on a troubled tone. "We know he's not just a myth now. He's real. He's a danger." Tarik replaced the weight with a clatter. "And we may never know who he's affected until it's too late."

Bas huffed out a breath. "That's worried me a bit too. But with the new shielding technology Sander's helped develop, I hope real protection is on the horizon. We've already begun implementing it here."

"Your quarters?" Tarik said sharply.

Bas looked down his nose at him. "No. I instructed the crews to begin with the larger public rooms, the places that expose the most people to danger."

"Bas—"

"Tarik." Bastien mocked Tarik's warning tone. "Allow me to make the decisions in my own home, if you please. My people's safety—"

"Is important. But so is yours. You're our king, Bas. You need to be safe too."

"But not at the expense of everyone near me." He gestured toward the door, silently inviting Tarik to accompany him. "As trying as our annual Bacchanalian holiday is, I encourage its excesses precisely because it reminds us—Royals and commoners alike—what happens when a monarch considers his own needs and wants more important than those of the people he was sworn to rule." He preceded Tarik into the private hallway that led to his quarters. "My own father, too, had difficulty remembering that diplomacy, policy, and good governance are our mandate, and not personal aggrandizement and superpowered showboating."

"You're not your father," Tarik said, buffeting Bas's shoulder, "and you're not the Mad King, no matter what's going through that perfectly groomed head of yours."

"I certainly try not to be. Although the opposition forces, both official parliamentary and unofficial rabble, might disagree."

"Parliament can kiss my ass," Tarik growled. "At least you're free from them for a couple of weeks."

"You'd think." Bastien led Tarik into his sitting room and tossed his robe onto a green-and-gold brocade armchair. All official governmental business was put on hold during Bonfire Fortnight in remembrance of the anarchy of the original events when Louis IV tried to dismantle Parliament. But with Parliament in recess during the entire two-week celebration, they had nothing better to do than poke their noses in Bas's personal business. "Yet they remain underfoot, and since Bonfire Fortnight requires New Palace hospitality and complete transparency on the part of the monarch, I can hardly order them to vacate the premises."

Tarik threw himself into another overly embroidered wingback chair next to the marble-mantled fireplace. "I could do it for you. I bet Gaston would help. Just say the word and they're gone."

Bas shook his head. "If I did that, I really *would* be following in the Mad King's footsteps." He glanced at Tarik, who was staring broodily into the fire. *Dare I tell him?* Nobody knew the truth. At least Bastien had never told anybody the truth, although God only knew who his father had admitted into his confidence—especially when he'd over-imbibed in his favorite Royal Crest port.

He trusted Tarik more than he trusted anybody in the world. Sharing his burden might make it easier for him to bear. *But I couldn't do that to him.* Bombarded with messages that caused his head to ache constantly unless he was surrounded by water or safe in his husband's arms, Tarik had enough to bear. Bas had no right to burden him with his own shameful secret as well.

He donned his most urbane smile. "In any case, it's not as though the esteemed MPs have anything new to say."

"They're not on you about that fucking betrothal contract again, are they?" Bas simply raised an eyebrow and Tarik groaned. "I thought that was scotched years ago."

Bastien, still not bothering to don a shirt, sauntered over to his desk under the window. The Prime Minister had delivered a fresh copy of the blasted contract yesterday, evidence of the shackles his father had fashioned when Bas was nothing more than a child. The gold seal at the bottom of the long parchment page glowed in the light from the rising sun, and its green ribbons fluttered in the chill breeze from the open window.

Bas shivered, and not because of the draft. He shut the window and plucked the document off the desk. "It's not dead yet, despite my best efforts." He crossed the room and released it to flutter into Tarik's lap. "They're reminding me of it once again, and this time, I might have to listen."

Tarik frowned at the document. "Your father was a fucking dinosaur. I can't believe he'd do this to you."

"Our relationship wasn't what you'd call warm." The older Bas got, and the more obvious it was that he wasn't the son his father had wanted, the colder Adélard had become.

Bas was only twenty-four when he took the throne. One of his first official acts as king was to take steps to break the contract, but bloody Parliament got involved and stalled the motion in committee. They were still skittish because Adélard had waited so long to get married and produce a legitimate heir. Bas hadn't fought it—at twenty-four, an enforced marriage at thirty-three seemed a lifetime away. Suddenly it was on his doorstep.

"Hold on." Tarik poked at the page with one finger. "It says here that the contract can be nullified by mutual agreement of both parties." He leaned back in his chair with a grin. "All you and Helena have to do is go before both Houses of Parliament and declare your intention not to marry and you're set."

Bas shot him a sour glance. "You're missing one or two salient points. First, what makes you think Helena will look the Prime Minister in the eye and say, 'Thank you very much, but I'd prefer not to be the queen consort.'"

Tarik's grin grew. "Getting a bit big for those perfectly pressed britches of yours, aren't you? You really think you're that irresistible?"

"It has nothing to do with *me*. It has to do with power and prestige. The Llívia title and estate are entailed to the male line. Once her father passes, everything goes to a distant cousin. This would be her chance to acquire some influence on her own."

"But aren't you forgetting something? She loathes you."

"Loathe is such a strong word." He lifted an eyebrow. "Besides, if I recall the—" He shuddered. "—the *frog* incident correctly, *you* were the one who cut off her hair, not me."

"She wouldn't have dropped the frog down your shirt in the first place if she actually liked you."

"You were there. The damn thing practically *leaped* down my shirt as though it had mistaken me for a lily pad."

Tarik snickered. "Just your luck to run into a supo who can communicate with animals." He tossed the contract onto the tea table. "My sister-in-law has a similar power, although hers isn't restricted to non-mammals."

"I suppose I should be glad it wasn't a snake." Bas shivered again. He really could *not* when it came to snakes. "Helena would probably be an excellent queen consort, if one had a taste for velvet bear traps."

"What do you mean?"

"Father insisted on inviting the Reys to visit for two weeks at least once a year."

Tarik nodded, a sour twist to his mouth. "He did that with our family too."

"He did it with everyone who had any influence and spent their entire visit demonstrating in subtle but invidious ways why it was to their advantage to support him and his policies and to turn a blind eye to his peccadilloes." Bastien sat in the wingback chair opposite Tarik and steepled his fingers. "So Helena and I were thrown together for the most miserable fourteen days of our years, right up until I turned eighteen and went to university. I made sure my holidays did not coincide with the Reys' visits."

"All the more reason for her to agree to the… the…" Tarik checked the document again. "The Repudiation."

"One of the things I discovered during those visits was that Helena is *very* good at getting her way, and not only with newts and salamanders."

"Persuasive, is she?"

"You accuse me of being Machiavellian. I'm convinced she's more Borgia-esque. Although with an impenetrable Princess Diana veneer. The thing is, nobody else seemed to notice it except me. Everyone else is convinced she's a paragon, and perfect for me."

"And you disagree?"

"For one thing, Tarik, in case you've forgotten, although I'm attracted more to a person than a gender, I tend to prefer men as sexual partners. For another, I have no desire to shackle myself to somebody who spends their entire time in my presence eyeing me as though they're considering how best to dispose of my body. I get enough of that from Parliament."

"So you're just going to go along with...with..." He tilted his head and peered down at the contract. "Getting engaged by your thirty-third birthday." He picked it up and squinted at the fine print above the seal. "So what happens if you don't get engaged? It doesn't say."

"I assume Parliament could introduce a motion to depose me."

"Not likely. The only reason for deposing a monarch is either egregious crimes, like our dear Louis, or insufficient superpowers."

Bastien froze, not responding, because his words were stuck in some alternate dimension, one in which he wasn't a sham and a failure.

Tarik looked away from the flames dancing on the grate —*like the flames of a bonfire, lit to consume a monstrous king*— and met Bas's no doubt bleak gaze. "Bas? What is it? I know damn well you're a good king. Far better than your father ever was. You certainly don't flaunt your powers like he did, but you were calibrated at puberty, same as all the rest of us were."

"No. I wasn't."

Tarik blinked at him. "What? But all Royals have to go through that if they want a place at court, and your place is the courtiest of all."

Bastien swallowed. *This is it.* "Father blocked it."

"But why? It's not as if it's a big deal."

"It is if..." Bas swallowed again, wishing for a bottle of Royal Crest port—or maybe a case—for a little over-imbibing of his own. "...if you don't have any powers. None befitting a Royal, anyway, least of all a king."

Tarik goggled at him, slowly straightening until his spine could have doubled for the fireplace poker. "You don't?" he croaked. "But...but..."

"Yes. *But*." Bastien sighed. "Do you plan to denounce me in the Upper House? Demand that I be deposed in favor of Anatole?" His cousin had been next in line for the throne until he turned eighteen, thanks to Adélard's dilatory approach to legal marriage and siring an heir. "You'd be within your rights."

"Fuck that. And fuck Anatole, that smug, smarmy bastard. He'd be a *terrible* king."

"My sentiments exactly. Which is why I've been assiduously avoiding the Calibration Ceremony since Father's death. But there's a new North Abarran Minister of Powers, risen up the ranks from the accounting department, apparently, and he's bringing a bean-counter's persistence to his job." Bas smiled wanly. "He's been after me for months, although he's treating it as an oversight due to the deplorable lack of efficiency under the previous minister rather than a deliberate act of treason on my part."

"It's not—" Tarik began hotly.

"I'm knowingly wielding authority to which I'm not entitled, contrary to our constitution. Isn't that the definition of treason?"

"It's stupid. A constitutional requirement that the monarch be superpowered? It's archaic. A holdover from the Schism, when we expected the monarchs of both countries to meet in personal combat."

"Nevertheless, it's still codified in our most basic laws." Bas's jaw clenched. "I should really turn *myself* in. But I've held onto the vain hope that good governance and attention to the needs of our people would outweigh the need for me to perform parlor tricks on demand."

"Bas—"

"I'm sorry." He scrubbed his hands through his hair, although it didn't disarrange the dark waves in the least. "I shouldn't have told you. Now you're complicit—"

"Fuck that. Now you've got somebody to help you find a solution." Tarik's brows drew together in an expression as fierce as a hawk's. "And we *will* find a solution. I'm surprised Uncle Adélard didn't find one himself."

"I believe his method of finding a solution was to attempt to get another heir, but my mother never quickened again, and Parliament wouldn't countenance a divorce." Bas let his head drop against the chair back. "Father's own fault for waiting until he was fifty to wed."

"So that was his solution? Replace you?"

"Well, that and the betrothal contract."

"How was that supposed to help?"

"As to that, we're back to the illustrious Mad King."

"Fuck." Tarik slumped in his chair. "Paired powers? He really went there?"

"Yes. Although I don't think Father really understood Louis's issues as well as he believed. Louis wouldn't have deflowered quite so many Royal maidens and discarded them like orange rinds if simply mating someone would do the trick. He never found anybody to replace his first queen."

"Bastard never stopped trying, though," Tarik grumbled.

"Exactly. He never stopped trying because he never found another compatible power to enhance his like hers did. Tying me to some random Royal isn't going to magically activate my powers. It has to be a specific person. A yin to my yang, as it were."

"And I'm guessing Helena isn't your idea of a yin."

"Not on your well-used married ass."

A knock sounded at the door. "Excuse me. Your Grace?"

Tarik turned to face the door. "Ah, Nico. Did you need me?"

Bastien straightened up. It was one thing to lounge in front of Tarik, but another thing altogether to appear slovenly in front of somebody else, even Tarik's—*holy mother of God.*

Bastien hastily stood and took the two strides toward the fireplace. He'd seen Tarik's assistant, Nico Pereira, on more than one occasion. But apparently he'd never *looked* at him before. Because surely he'd have remembered if he'd ever seen him in those wire-framed *glasses*.

Wavy brown hair, straight nose that would be cute if it weren't bordering on forceful, clear hazel eyes, currently gazing at him wide-eyed behind those bloody adorable *glasses*.

But Bastien would resist this sudden tug of attraction, because he wasn't the Mad King and he didn't take advantage of his subjects—no matter how enticing they were in their goddamned *glasses*.

CHAPTER TWO

"I— I beg your pardon, Your Grace, Your Majesty." Nico couldn't tear his eyes away from the king. Who wasn't wearing a shirt. "Baroness Savatier told me I could find you here, but—"

The king. Isn't wearing a shirt.

His Grace of Arles—whom Nico usually managed to think of as *Tarik*, as the duke had requested, except when distracted because ohmygod, *the king wasn't wearing a shirt* —motioned for Nico to enter the sitting room. "No trouble, Nico. What's up?"

Other than the king being half-naked? "Um, I've got the commemorative corkscrew for you to use at the ceremony this afternoon."

"Ceremony?" King Bastien turned around, and Nico tried not to swallow his tongue at the sight of the royal pecs—but it was a struggle. "What ceremony?"

Tarik grinned up at the king, apparently unaffected by the sight of all that smooth, golden skin and defined muscle. *Of course he's unaffected. The king is his cousin. He's probably seen this sight hundreds of times. And besides, he's married to one of the buffest men in both Abarras.* "You've forgotten, haven't you?"

King Bastien looked down his nose at Tarik. "I don't *forget* things, *mon cousin*. I merely offload everything but the most pressing details to external memory."

"External memory?" Tarik raised an obviously skeptical brow. "I didn't realize you'd achieved true cyborg status, Bas."

Nico cleared his throat. "I, uh, think His Majesty is referring to his private secretary. Mr. Vidal keeps His Majesty's calendar and handles his correspondence."

"Ah, right." Tarik crossed his feet at the ankles. "Since the estimable Vidal hasn't downloaded your schedule for today, I'll remind you." Although he didn't take his gaze off the king—*and who could blame him*—Tarik held out his hand, and Nico placed the engraved platinum corkscrew in his palm. "Today is the official tasting ceremony for Royal Roses Red Blend, the collaboration between the Royal Crest vineyards and Roses Estate."

Was that a blush staining the king's cheeks? If so, it vanished immediately—not that Nico was looking. *Uh huh. Right.* "Of course. Sander's and your birthday gift to me."

"Exactly."

"A formal ceremony?"

Tarik snorted. "What do you think? It's a joint venture between North and South Abarra. Another chink in the wall between our countries."

"Definitely formal then."

"Formal doesn't have to be painful, Bas, you twit. You'll let me open a bottle and pour you a glass. All you have to do is drink the damn wine."

A smile tugged at the king's lips, a fond expression that Nico had only been privileged to see a handful of times, and usually in company with Tarik. He glanced down at himself. "Then I expect my current attire will be unsuitable. I'd best take a shower before I'm reminded of some other obligation."

"Shower? Why bother? It's not as if you need it."

Nico's brain whited out for a moment and an image arose, obscuring his view of the room. *The king. Naked. And wet.* He lost his grip on his tablet and despite fumbling to catch it, it headed straight for the sharp edge of the marble table in front of the fire. "Crap!"

At the last possible moment, King Bastien lunged forward and must have somehow batted the tablet aside, because it plopped onto the overstuffed cushion of a heavily brocaded chair. The king picked it up and held it out to Nico. "Crisis averted, eh?"

A crisis I didn't see coming. Nico accepted the tablet, and although his fingers brushed the king's, he couldn't really enjoy it. Because he'd just experienced yet another example of why his stupid, secret, *illegal* power was worthless.

What good was foresight unless you could actually foresee something useful? *Other than the king. Naked.*

"Th-thank you, Your Majesty. I apologize for being so clumsy."

"Nonsense." He waved one elegant, long-fingered hand. "It could happen to anybody."

"Anybody except you," Tarik grumbled. "When was the last time you dropped something?"

"If you're not careful, I'll drop something on you," the king said testily. "Perhaps a brick. On your head."

Tarik pushed himself out of his chair. "Is that any way to treat someone who's giving you such an awesome birthday gift? Just wait until you taste this wine, Bas. It's incredible." He grinned at Nico. "Isn't that right, Nico?"

Nico blinked, reluctantly banishing a momentary vision of the king stepping into the shower because that ass was even more mesmerizing than his chest. "Oh. Yes. Quite, Your Grace."

Tarik shot him an admonitory look. "If you're *Your Gracing* me again, you either disapprove of what I'm doing or have something else on your mind."

Nico's eyes widened in panic. Surely the duke's powers didn't include mind-reading. For one thing, mind control powers were illegal. Even though telepathy was a gray area, it still required consent. But Nico had never had a hint that Tarik could intercept *thoughts* as well as airborne transmissions. *A good thing, too.* Because Nico's inappropriate crush on the king was the last thing he wanted to share with anybody, let alone his boss—who just happened to be the king's best friend as well as cousin.

Denying the danger is the best I can do. "Yes, Your Grace. I have a few more details to address before the ceremony begins. Do you want me to send you the usual fifteen-minute warning?" Nico needed a cell phone to send the message, but Tarik didn't need anything but his mind to receive it.

"Probably a good idea. Although..." He frowned meditatively. "Since Sander's arriving shortly, there's a good chance I might not receive it." He slid a sidelong glance at the king.

"Kindly spare us the details of what you and your husband get up to, if not for my sake, then for poor Nico's." The king inclined his head at Nico. "Thank you, Nico. And you needn't worry. I'll make sure he arrives on time."

"Yeah, but who's going to make sure *you* arrive on time?" Tarik asked with a leer.

"Vidal, of course." He nodded at Nico again. "You may go."

Nico scuttled out of the room, leaving the king and the duke bickering good naturedly. He barely registered the increasing traffic in the New Palace hallways as he sped out of the residential wing and into the more public spaces.

I saw the king naked. Granted, he'd only seen him fully naked in a vision, and only a flicker of one at that, but Nico's visions were never that... that *specific*. Or detailed. *The curve of the king's muscular backside, the water sluicing over his wide shoulders and down his spine.* Gah!

Nico stumbled over nothing, earning him an irritated glance from a passing MP. Usually, his foresight simply directed his attention to some article necessary for his duties —like last night, when he was preparing for today's ceremony and got a flash of the corkscrew sitting on the corner of Tarik's desk back at the Royal Crest offices.

He'd never had a...a *voyeur* vision before. Ugh. He needed to be more careful about how he framed his *need-to-know* nudges to his annoying power.

Although the sight of the king *naked*... He stumbled again and this time bumped into one of the provincial barons whose name Nico couldn't remember. "Sorry. Sorry."

The baron stared at Nico coldly before brushing off his sleeve as if contact with someone as lowly as a vineyard manager might contaminate his overly ornate scarlet uniform.

Nico peered around at the rotunda inside the main palace doors. Wow. He'd noticed that things were a little busier, but the palace was always a hive of activity during the day. This throng, though, was *extra*.

The crowd parted, and he glimpsed Her Majesty, Queen Genevieve—the beloved *Queen Mum*—presenting her cheek to be kissed by an extraordinarily beautiful dark-haired woman whom Nico recognized from Tarik and Sander's wedding: Lady Helena Rey. Her parents, the Duke and Duchess of Llívia, stood on either side of her, beaming as Queen Genevieve spoke to them animatedly, her dainty hands sketching patterns in the air.

Prince Anatole, the current Heir Presumptive, since King Bastien hadn't yet produced progeny of his own, strode through the doors and posed as if he were standing in his own personal mental spotlight. Overdressed, as usual, and his retinue of toadies wasn't much better. At least the Reys adopted an understated elegance that declared their quality far better than the prince's ostentatious display.

Overcompensating. It was definitely a thing.

When another retinue boiled through the doors, crowding Prince Anatole out of center stage, as it were, Nico decided that he needed a little space—and relief from Royals. As devoted as he was to Tarik, and as much as he admired King Bastien and the Queen Mum, when the rest of the North Abarran Royals got together, they were officially *too fricking much.*

He dodged out of the main rotunda and took a detour through the service corridors to the executive wing of the New Palace, where the king's offices—and more to the point, the king's private secretary's office—were located. When he popped out of the door between the two burnished suits of armor belonging to the Northern princes who fought in the Schism that split old Abarra into North and South, he almost popped back in again.

Because *whoops!* The new Minister of Powers for North Abarra was striding down the center of the deep gold carpet, and though his feet made no noise on the plush pile, it was clear he was stomping.

The last thing Nico wanted was to draw the Minister's attention. If commoners with illegal powers had learned anything during their training at the Municipal, it was to fly so far under the Ministry's radar as to be invisible. And Nico had heard stories about the new Minister—he wasn't as lazy or complacent as his predecessor. Any hint of the type of powers that so many commoners wielded could be enough to start another Great Purge.

Yes, thank you, Mad King, for that little legacy too.

Nico would be more than happy to cast his official Louis IV effigy into the flames on Bonfire Night.

But a sure way to draw attention was to act guilty. So Nico forced himself to walk calmly out the door. After all, he was the personal assistant to a Royal duke—it was completely expected for him to use the service corridors. He simply nodded respectfully to the Minister as he headed toward his goal. *Nothing to see here.*

He shot a final glance at the Minister's retreating back and then ducked inside the door and shut it behind him so he could collapse against it.

Corin Vidal, Nico's best friend since their days training for royal administration at the Municipal, was sitting behind his desk, the glow from his massive monitor shifting subtly over his brown skin and tight curls as a document flashed by on the screen. Corin paused the display with a click of his mouse.

"Nico? What's the matter?"

"Matter?" Nico squeaked. *I saw the king naked.* "The Royal hordes, what else?"

Corin wrinkled his nose. "Ugh. Don't remind me. Bonfire Fortnight is the *worst*. All of them milling around underfoot for the whole two weeks, playing one-upmanship with each other and getting their noses out of joint if they think they haven't been accorded proper reverence." Corin stood and stretched. "I mean, they're all right in small doses, but in a mass like this—"

"They're beastly," they both said together.

Corin chuckled and gestured toward the cozy seating area next to his own fireplace. A tea service was resting on the round marble table, and a triple-tiered tray of the palace chef's famous scones sat next to it. "Come have some breakfast."

"I had breakfast two hours ago." But he crossed the room nevertheless. "And so did you, I'll wager. You never slept past five-thirty, even when you weren't the exalted private secretary to the king."

Corin grinned. "Second breakfast, then. Besides, it's always time for scones." He waggled his eyebrows. "Lemon ginger today."

"Say no more." Nico abandoned his own tablet on the credenza against the wall under a vast tapestry depicting the D'Aramitz coat of arms. He sat down opposite Corin, the wingback chairs comfortable and not nearly so ornate as the ones in the king's sitting room. *Where he wasn't wearing a shirt.*

Crap. Nico grabbed a scone and stuffed half of it in his mouth. He needed to get a grip. He respected King Bastien completely. He was an excellent king, firmly committed to the welfare of his people and the country, even if—or maybe especially if—it meant challenging long-held biases about rivalry with the South. He *never* exercised his powers in an attempt to intimidate both allies and adversaries the way King Adélard had done.

And yes, he'd noticed that the king was handsome—hard to miss when his picture was on all the money—but he'd seen him as more an icon than a flesh-and-blood man. Now that he'd seen the flesh, though…

He'd had no notion that the king would be so…so *fit*. The breadth of his shoulders in all those formal uniforms—even the ones without epaulettes—not to mention the trim waist and narrow hips, should have given Nico a clue.

Now? He couldn't *unsee* any of that. *I am so screwed.* But at least his interactions with the king were few and brief. Once Bonfire Fortnight was over, Nico would return to the vineyard, doing his job, and *not thinking* about the king naked. At all. Ever.

"Nico?" Corin's amused tone brought Nico's head up. His friend's eyes twinkled at him over the rim of his teacup. "Is there something you'd like to share with the class?"

"What? No. Why?"

"Because you've just consumed three scones in such rapid succession that I'm surprised you didn't choke, and the crumbs from a fourth are scattered around your feet like lemon-ginger snowflakes."

Nico glanced at the floor. Sure enough, one of the chef's delectable scones was nothing but savory rubble around his oxfords. "Sorry. I'll clean it up."

Corin waved Nico back into his seat. "Leave it for later. I'll hit it with the cordless vac before the cleaning staff can see it and wonder who let the Neanderthals in. I repeat. What's up?"

No way could Nico admit to perving on Corin's boss. They shared most things—Corin was aware of Nico's limited foresight, just as Nico knew all about Corin's photographic memory and seemingly limitless reading speed. But that detail would have to remain secret.

"Just stress. I haven't been around this many Royals at one time since Tarik and Sander's wedding."

Corin shook his head. "I can't believe you call them by their first names."

"They insist." He smirked a little, because Corin was the one person he could count on to understand. "Addressing them by title is how I show disapproval."

Corin grinned. "And nobody can give you shit about disrespect because you're being entirely proper. Nice."

"Do you..." He swallowed, mouth dry from so many scones, and snatched up the tea Corin had poured for him. "How do you address the king?"

"Other than *Your Majesty*?" Corin asked dryly.

"Well. Yes. I mean, you work so closely with him. He calls you his external memory."

Corin's eyebrows shot up, and pleasure flickered across his face. "He does? How do you know?"

"I heard him. Just now. I had to take the ceremonial corkscrew to Tarik and His Majesty was there." Nico stared into his teacup and mumbled, "Without his shirt."

Corin must have been in the process of sipping his tea because he choked, tea spurting out his nose and onto his gray trousers. When Nico jumped up to help, Corin motioned him down again. "I'm all right. I—" He coughed and mopped his face with a linen napkin. "God, no wonder you're all discombobulated."

"I'm not!" Nico slumped in the chair. "Okay, maybe a little. But you've got to admit—"

"He's a lot," Corin said. "Although it's probably the contrast that's the shocker. I mean, he's never anything but perfectly groomed and pristinely dressed. You can't even imagine him *en dishabille*."

"I can," Nico muttered to his tea. "Unfortunately." *And it's so not the contrast.* It was definitely *him*. In the Magisterial flesh.

"Well, never mind. Are you set for the tasting ceremony? Do you need any help?"

"I've got everything set, although if you could make sure both the king and the dukes arrive on time? Every stinking Royal in the place will be there, since it's the official kick-off for the Bonfire Fortnight festivities."

"And none of them could bear to not be invited. Their status would suffer. Even though we're only watching His Majesty drink a little wine."

"Hey!" Nico sat up, his professional pride stung. "It's an *incredible* wine. The best out of either vineyard for years."

"Do the other Royals get a taste?"

Nico's smile wasn't at all nice. He could tell by the way Corin's expression reflected it. "We'll have cases available. Which we'll be happy to distribute, provided a suitably generous donation is given to the dukes' designated charity."

Corin's chuckle was downright evil. "I like it. Forcing them to do a good deed while indulging their avarice and brown-nosing. What's the charity?"

The office door burst open. "Hello!"

Nico startled, his teacup rattling in the saucer, although he didn't drop his in his lap like Corin did.

Standing in the doorway in worn hiking boots and a canvas duster, her dark hair skewered into a messy bun by what seemed to be a Sharpie, was Her Royal Highness, Princess Katalin Fiala of Roses. She was smiling at them both, and when Princess Katalin smiled, you couldn't help but smile back—unless, of course, you were a hard-line Separatist. Because Princess Katalin was the niece of the Queen of *South* Abarra, and her essential free run of the North Abarran New Palace shoved a stick even further up the Separatists' collective ass.

But Princess Katalin and King Bastien had become fast friends during their stint as wedding godparents for Tarik and Sander, her brother. And now…

"Corin, meet the representative of the dukes' chosen charity—the New Abarran Animal Rescue League."

Princess Katalin beamed at them both. Since she was wearing her field gear, she must be inhabiting her Anime persona: Her power was communicating with animals, and her grandfather had bestowed the moniker on her when she was only seven. She was remarkable not only for her ability to communicate with any animal (although she said insects were beyond her), but for how early her powers manifested.

And also because she was a genuinely nice person.

"Isn't it cool? I've spent the last three months helping to set up clinics all over North Abarra." She wrinkled her nose. "And let me tell you, some of your Northern gentry need to lighten the heck up. We're talking rescuing puppies and kittens! Doggies and kitties! Not an armed invasion of drooling zombies."

Nico laughed. "They'll come around." Corin and the princess both stared at him skeptically. "Well, maybe not the gentry. But the commoners. This is something that's sorely needed here, so the Royals can suck it up and shell out the bucks."

"Exactly." Katalin bit her lip. "But here's the thing…" She glanced between the two of them, her expression almost apologetic. "I can't stay for the tasting ceremony."

"What?" Nico set his teacup down before he dropped it. "But you agreed to introduce the charity."

Corin was still blotting his pants with a napkin. "We were counting on your charm to part the Royals from their ducats."

She laughed. "Oh, Bastien has charm enough for that." She winked. *A princess who winked?* "For that matter, the two of you are no slouches in that department either."

Nico shared a somewhat panicked glance with Corin. "I'm sure we'd never presume to influence—"

"Relax, boys. I've grown up with court politics. I'm perfectly aware that staff are just as influential—and usually more effective—than the Royals they serve. You've met Luken, my brother's valet-slash-factotum. I'm convinced he could rule the world if he wanted to."

"Quite," Nico croaked. Luken was almost twenty years older than he and Corin, but his reputation lived on at the Municipal. Princess Katalin was more accurate than she knew.

"Anywaaay…" She grimaced. "The Conservancy's called me in on an emergency orangutan retrieval and I've got to leave, like, two hours ago. The actual rescue shouldn't take long. I just have to convince the poor little thing that she'll be safe with the conservation team. It's the travel." She rolled her eyes. "Borneo is not the easiest place to reach. But I'd never miss Bas's birthday. I'll be back by then."

"We understand, Your Highness," Corin said with a slight bow.

"Oh, please," she said with another eye roll. "It's Kat. Just Kat."

"Your Highness"—Nico began but cleared his throat at her glower—"*Kat*. We can't be so informal with you. We'd be reprimanded by Baroness Savatier for lack of proper respect."

"Say no more." She grimaced. "Your Chamberlain puts the fear of God into me. But I'm warning you—I'll suffer the indignity in public, but here, when it's just us? We're friends. And friends can drop the stupid formalities, right?"

Nico smiled at her, because she really was delightful. "Of course. Kat."

She beamed. "That's better." She bit her lip again. "Sooo, friends can ask for favors, right?"

"Uh…yes?" Nico said.

Kat reached into her capacious duster pocket and pulled out…

"Is that a tribble?" Corin asked.

"Don't be ridiculous," she scoffed. "Tribbles aren't real. It's a kitten." She held the little ball of orange, black, and white fluff in her cupped palms and it uncurled to reveal that yes, it was a kitten, who blinked wide green eyes at them all. "I found her stuck in a drainpipe outside the palace walls, and I don't have time to go back to the shelter and hand her over to the staff there."

The kitten's eyes narrowed and her rather oversized ears flicked back. Nico retreated a pace, as did Corin. But Kat just cocked an eyebrow at the kitten. "I told you that you couldn't come with me. These two lovely gentlemen will take excellent care of you until I come back."

"Us?" Corin squeaked. "We can't—"

"She's a kitten," Kat said patiently. "Not a Tasmanian devil or a time bomb." She cut a glance at the kitten, whose ears had flattened further. "Not if she knows what's good for her." The kitten shot one hind foot out and licked her toes, her tiny claws poking out between orange fur tufts. "She'll behave. Although it would be best if she stayed with one of you all the time. I can't vouch for her if she's left without supervision." The kitten stopped grooming her foot and glared at Kat, her pink tongue protruding as if she'd forgotten to reel it in. Kat gave her a stern look. "You *did* get stuck in a drainpipe, so I think my concerns are perfectly valid." She thrust the kitten at Nico. "Here. Her name's Polita."

"You named her?" Nico took the kitten gingerly.

"Of course not. She named herself. It means 'pretty' in Basque." Kat shrugged. "I never said she was modest."

Nico squeaked as Polita swarmed up his arm, leaving a trail of pulled threads in one of his best blazers. He was half-afraid she'd continue her climb, and those claws might be small, but they were clearly sharp. Instead of continuing to the top of his head or going for his eyes, though, she plopped down on his shoulder, nestled against his neck in a tickle of soft fur. And began to purr.

"There, see?" Kat said triumphantly. "She likes you. You'll be fine." She wagged a finger at them—Nico, Corin, and presumably Polita as well. "Just don't let her bamboozle you. She doesn't need to get her way all the time."

Polita's mew in Nico's ear sounded remarkably like the feline equivalent of *Ha!*

CHAPTER THREE

Bas studied his reflection in the triple mirrors in his dressing room and sighed. Although the uniform fit him perfectly and was in impeccable condition—as usual—he wished he wouldn't be trapped in formal clothing for the next two weeks. Bonfire Fortnight, while it was a holiday for the rest of the country and all the elected governmental officials, meant that the monarch was on near-constant display. The echo of his father's words played in Bas's head: *Appearances must be maintained.*

"Appearances," Bas murmured to his reflection, "are a bloody pain in the ass."

His dressing room sat between his bedroom and his private sitting room, adjacent to his bathroom. With one last unnecessary smoothing of his hair, he entered the sitting room, knowing that household staff would have timed the tea tray perfectly once the inexplicable New Palace gossip mill picked up and transmitted the news that he'd stepped into the shower.

I'm so predictable that they can time my shower and dressing down to the minute. His tailored clothing never needed attention—although the staff regularly cleaned them for form's sake, if nothing else. But he was a grown man. He didn't need any help putting on his trousers, for God's sake. He still had a valet technically on staff, but Carstairs had been his father's valet, and was elderly enough to appreciate the lightened-to-the-point-of-non-existent duties. Yet even in the absence of a personal servant, the staff always knew when he was ready to greet the day.

The cup of tea on the marble table next to the fireplace was still wreathed in steam, but the room was empty. He glanced at the clock on the mantelpiece. Vidal—Corin—should be here any moment to go over today's schedule. Undoubtedly there would be other events after the tasting ceremony.

I wonder if Nico will be there in his glasses?

Bas's cock twitched, and he ordered it to stand down as he took a gulp of scalding tea. "Blast!"

"Now, darling, is that any way to greet your mother?"

Bas set his cup down, slowly and carefully, to give his misbehaving genitals a chance to recover. Then he turned to greet Genevieve. "Mother." He held out his hands, and she floated over to him, still as graceful as she'd always been. Her slow mental decline hadn't affected her physically at least. He bent to kiss her cheek. "If I'd known you were here, I'd have curbed my unruly tongue."

She smiled up at him, her hands resting on his chest below the double row of medals. She only came up to his breastbone, a tiny, fairylike woman. "I know you better than that, silly boy. But you always apologize so beautifully that I never mind."

"Won't you sit, Mother? I've tea here, and I don't expect Co— Vidal for another few minutes if you'd like to join me in a cup."

"No, no, darling. I have to be..." Her brow wrinkled, her eyes growing distant. "Never mind. I'm sure Rozenn told me, but it's slipped my mind."

"Mother—"

"I'll just pop along to the Blue Room and check in with her again."

The Blue Room hadn't been blue for seven years, repurposed from a public space to private family quarters after Bas had finally pushed through his plans for New Palace renovation and turned it into a solarium.

Bas covered her hands with his own. "Mother, let me call the baroness for you. She'd doubtless be happy to meet you here." The Crown's Chamberlain, Baroness Savatier of Montferrar, had come to the palace with Genevieve when she became Queen Consort. She still called the baroness by her first name, Rozenn.

"Nonsense, nonsense. She'll find me when she's ready." She blinked. "When I'm ready. When it's time." She blinked again, and her eyes cleared. "I wanted to speak to you, darling. About that dreadful little man who's been positively *haunting* the Palace for *weeks*."

"What dreadful little man is that?" Bas held his breath, hoping she could come up with a name. Her hands twitched under his as though she wanted to wave his question away.

"Oh, you must have seen him. He has those silly muttonchop whiskers, but no hair at all on his head. And the most dreadful taste in waistcoats."

"You mean the Minister of Powers?" he said, holding his humor at bay. He wondered how Léon Neuville, one of the most starched-up bureaucrats Bas had ever met, would react to being described as a *dreadful little man*.

"I suppose. Anyway, could you do me the greatest favor, darling?"

He kissed her cheek again. "I'd do anything for you, *ma mère.* You know that."

"Then would you please do whatever it is he wants so he'll get out from underfoot? I don't want him spoiling your birthday celebrations."

Bas's smile froze. What Léon wanted was to calibrate Bas's powers, and Bas couldn't afford for that to happen.

Not if he wanted to remain king. And since the next in line for the throne should he be deposed was his cousin Anatole, the most narcissistic horse's ass in both Abarras, Bas couldn't do that to his people, to his country. "I'm not sure —"

"I told him you would take care of it before the party. It can't be anything more than a formality, after all. Once it's done, we can relax and enjoy the festivities without him sending doleful looks our way every five minutes and casting a positive *gloom* over everything."

"Mother—"

"Now." She leaned closer and lowered her voice to a conspiratorial whisper. "I've got a surprise for you. A wonderful surprise."

He matched her tone. "Is it a pony?"

She laughed, light and musical as ever. "No, silly. Of course not. You're far too big for a pony." She drew her hands out from under his and turned toward the open door. "You can come in now, dear."

Lady Helena Rey stepped into the room and offered him a nod just this side of respectful. "Hello, Your Majesty."

"Lady Helena," he ground out between teeth clenched in a brittle smile. "I hadn't realized your family had arrived. Welcome to the New Palace."

Genevieve clasped her hands under her chin. "Isn't she lovely? As pretty as a picture. Just perfect."

Bastien had never been able to understand why everyone gushed so about Helena's looks. She was certainly a well-enough looking woman. Her brown hair was always arranged in an attractive style—at least once she'd recovered from the unfortunate haircut Tarik had given her in retaliation for the frog incident. Her couturier was a genius, her clothes always styled with understated elegance. But her complexion, so lauded in the popular press as putting damask roses and cream to shame, had never seemed more than ordinary to him. *Nico's skin is more alluring.*

But maybe that was the difference. Bas had never been attracted to her as a person, and while he could appreciate Helena's beauty in the abstract, it simply didn't move him the way it apparently moved the many would-be poets who wrote paeans to her face.

Genevieve apparently wasn't aware of the chilliness that fairly crystalized the air between him and Helena. "I know you two would love to chat before the announcement."

Bas's attention snapped to his mother. "Announcement?"

She twinkled at him and patted his arm. "No need to be coy, darling. I'm your mother, after all. I'll just leave you two alone for a few minutes."

"Mother—"

But she was gone, flitting out the door in a swish of violet silk skirts.

Bas sighed. "May I offer you a cup of tea, Helena? It's fresh."

She shut the door firmly and then strolled further into the room. "With no one about but you and me, I believe it may be time for a frank discussion." She favored him with a wintry smile. "However, I won't say no to a cup. Milk. No sugar."

As Bas prepared her tea, she settled herself gracefully in the chair Tarik had so recently occupied. He wished fervently for Tarik to return. He was possibly the only person in the country whose distaste for Helena exceeded his own.

I'm the blasted king. Surely I can stand up for myself against one of my own subjects.

She accepted the cup. "Thank you. I realize this situation is not one either of us would have chosen, but it's past time for us to put aside our old hurts and discuss the situation like reasonable Royals." She took a dainty sip. "For the sake of the country if nothing else."

"I'm uncertain how many Royals can actually be termed *reasonable*." Bas sat opposite her and crossed his legs. "And I'm unaware of the situation to which you refer."

"As your mother said, don't be coy. You know what I'm talking about."

He steepled his fingers. "I assure you. I do not."

She sighed, her mouth turning down in highly unattractive disappointment. "I'm fully aware that you've been attempting to annul our betrothal contract for years."

"Nine years, seven months, to be exact. We don't suit, Helena. We never have, even as children."

"Bastien." Her tone was loaded with exasperation. "We're Royals. *High-ranking* Royals. We're fully aware of the exigencies of a politically advantageous arranged marriage. If you imagine I envision a love-match, you much mistake my heart."

"I doubt that very seriously, Helena." He favored her with his own wintry smile. *I'm not convinced you have one.*

She set her teacup aside. "Let me be perfectly clear, Bastien. I have been raised to be Queen Consort since our fathers signed that contract. I'm trained to rule, to govern, to be a political asset to you as king."

"But not to care for me as a man."

She shook her head, her expression almost indulgent. "You owe your existence to a political match. You more than anyone must understand that sentimentalities have little place for people of our rank."

"Sentimental or not, I believe that in order to rule our country effectively, it's necessary to care for its people. Which includes its king. I take it you will not repudiate the contract before Parliament."

She leaned back in her chair and rested her hands along its arms, her scarlet nails like blood splashed on the green and gold brocade. "I don't believe it's in anyone's best interest—yours, mine, or the country's, so no. I will not."

"Then I will continue my efforts to have the contract annulled."

"In a week? With Parliament in recess for Bonfire Fortnight? You've left it too long, Bastien. You're out of time. Accept the inevitable and announce the engagement today as your Mother wishes."

"I will not." Bastien matched Helena's exact tone and cadence.

She dropped her gaze, a wrinkle pleating the skin between her brows, and traced the pattern in the chair's fabric with one fingernail. "Given your own situation, perhaps you should reconsider. Having someone at your side to help you…deflect suspicion would be advantageous, don't you think?"

Adélard told her. He didn't keep the secret. Bas counted on his celebrated outward calm to hide his reaction. Judging by the irritation that flickered over her features, he was successful. He took a moment to push aside his anger at his father. Chances were that Adélard had told Ferran Rey, Helena's father, probably after too many glasses of port over their contract negotiations. But Ferran would have told his wife and daughter. If nothing else, the Reys had always presented a united front.

"I happen to believe that effective government doesn't require the threat of powered intimidation. Just because I don't choose to flaunt my power before the world doesn't mean it doesn't exist."

This time, her smile chilled him down to the bone. "An interesting perspective, if rather disingenuous." She rose gracefully to her feet. "I'll be ready for the announcement at the tasting ceremony. And you needn't worry, Bastien. I shan't embarrass either one of us."

He accompanied her across the room, carefully not brushing against her, and ushered her out of the room. After he closed the door behind her, he leaned against it and closed his eyes.

"Blast." Why hadn't he pushed Parliament harder on the annulment? He huffed a laugh and wandered over to the window to look down at the garden. He'd had his last futile argument with his father about the contract there, Adélard calmly peeling a tangerine as Bastien had paced in front of him.

"Of course I don't want you to be unhappy, my boy," Adélard had said, popping a tangerine section into his mouth. "I simply don't want you to go mad and start destroying all the stately homes in the country the way Louis did."

"Thank you, Father," Bas said dryly. "That's very comforting. But I believe Louis didn't start bombarding every castle in the country until after his wife died. Perhaps it would be better for me to remain single."

"Nonsense. A paired power will never be fully realized without a mate. If the Ministry of Powers should discover that your abilities are so... so..."

"So pathetically insignificant?"

"Well. Yes. They could invoke the old laws to have you deposed."

"Surely governing well is more important than how powered I am."

His father glowered. "Not to the Ministry. And certainly not to Parliament. You can't buck centuries of tradition. That Southern harridan, Maialen, can spawn dozens of ancillaries of herself. Her son is a *shapeshifter*, for God's sake. What do you suppose they'll say when they find out the only thing you can do is stay comfortable regardless of the temperature, keep your clothing neat, and avoid mosquito bites?"

"That I never sweat, always present a pristine appearance as befits a Royal, and don't scratch my ass in public?" Bas returned blandly. He was grateful for the first ability. It kept his father from seeing how truly terrified he was of following in the Mad King's footsteps.

"Don't be crass, Bastien."

"Really, Father, some of our ancestors never managed to meet even those very basic criteria. King Frederick III, for instance, never made it through a single Northern Hope Medal ceremony without digging at his crotch at least twice."

"The subject is closed, Bastien."

He'd stood up and strode off, leaving Bastien seething with helpless frustration—and leaving the tangerine peels for the staff to clean off the flagstones.

Bas sighed and placed one hand on the glass. "We're all still picking up after you, Father." And unless Bas could find some way out of this marriage, that would never change.

Nico surveyed the audience chamber that Baroness Savatier had set aside for the tasting ceremony. It was enormous, although not as vast as the ballroom where the ball marking the end of Bonfire Fortnight would be held. But the ballroom had to accommodate ballgowns, orchestra, and a dance floor. Today's ceremony only required standing room.

He nodded decisively. *It'll do.*

He scanned the stacks of wine crates, the entwined emblems of Royal Crest and Roses Estate stamped in purple ink on their slats. The Royals' donations should yield a more than respectable amount for Kat's animal rescue organization. He chuckled as he tweaked the gold-embroidered tablecloth straight and steadied the three balloon wineglasses etched with the D'Aramitz coat of arms —one for the king, one for Tarik, and one for Sander. Everything was in order. Nothing missing.

Suddenly, the gold-embroidered velvet tablecloth jerked sideways and began to slide off the end of the table, sending the glasses *tink*ing against one another.

"No!" Nico slapped his hands on the cloth, although it continued to twitch under his hands. He peered over the edge of the table and spotted a pair of floofy orange paws, their claws sunk into the plush green fabric. *Why didn't I insist Corin babysit the kitten?*

With one palm firmly flattened on the tablecloth, he reached down and disengaged Polita's claws. "You are a very bad cat," he muttered as she batted at his fingers. "Stop that."

She poked her head out from under the cloth, its gold fringe making her look as if she were wearing a gilded wig worthy of Queen Nefertiti. She blinked up at him and mewed. "And stop that too. Just because you're cute, you can't persuade me that you're sweet and innocent. You've already coated my trousers in fur, ruined my best blazer, and scattered paperclips all over Corin's office. Now you're apparently trying to get me fired."

She scrambled out from under the table, flicking her ridiculously fluffy tail as she peered around. Her ears flattened again, as if all his careful arrangements didn't meet her exacting standards.

"I suppose you'd do everything differently," he huffed and pointed at her. "Let me tell you, I've been at this job for —" He stared from his finger to the kitten, whose back had arched, orange and black fur standing up along her spine. She bounced sideways on all four feet and pounced on something on the carpet that had apparently offended her, paying no attention to Nico at all.

"What am I doing? She's a *cat*." Princess Katalin might be able to chat merrily with her, but Nico's powers didn't extend to forecasting the behavior of creatures that didn't subscribe to logic.

He sighed, scooping her up off the carpet to hold her in front of his face as Katalin had done. "Behave. Or I'll tell the princess on you." She just blinked innocently at him, all big eyes and tufted ears, as if she weren't the spawn of Satan.

He deposited her on top of one of the wine crates so he could straighten the tablecloth and rearrange the glasses. She wasn't fond of that—she patrolled the top of the crates, denouncing him with a decidedly outraged mew.

"Just a minute. I'll take you back to Corin's office and give you some nice tuna fish. You'd like that, wouldn't you?" He counted her more mollified mew as a *yes*. He tweaked the tablecloth so the fringe hit the carpet evenly all the way around and repositioned the wine glasses so they were centered exactly. *There*. Everything was perfect. Tarik could pull the wine bottle out of the open crate and—

The open crate.

He spun, scanning the shoulder-high wall of wine crates for Polita. Not there. *For God's sake, she's a cat. She can jump.* The tablecloth wasn't moving again, thank goodness, but—

He heard it then. The rustle of excelsior from beneath the table. Then, ominously, it stopped.

"Crap!" Nico scrabbled with the tablecloth, flipping it up and knocking the glasses on their sides with an ominous *clish*. Corin had called the housekeeping staff for a litter pan for Polita, but it hadn't arrived before Nico had to leave to prep for the ceremony. Despite coaxing from Corin, the kitten had refused to leave Nico's shoulder, as the puncture wounds on his neck attested. He looked as if he'd been attacked by the world's tiniest vampire.

But if she needed to...do her business and did it in the crate that held the specially labeled bottle of wine? *I'm so dead*. He couldn't let Tarik pour the king—the *king*—a glass of wine from a bottle covered in cat pee. It just wasn't *done*.

He yanked the crate from beneath the table, and breathed a sigh of relief. Polita was simply nestled amid the excelsior, curled into a little calico ball, fast asleep. He left her there for a moment so he could reposition the glasses *again*. "There. *Now* we're ready." If the wine bottle sported one or two threads of cat fur, nobody would see. "Let's hope the king isn't allergic to cats, or things could get awkward." Polita, unsurprisingly, ignored him. "At least now we've got everything we need so—"

A flash of platinum against gray-veined white marble obscured his eyesight. *The corkscrew*. He recognized the marble too—the table in the king's sitting room that had almost been the death of Nico's tablet. Damn it, Tarik must have forgotten it *again*.

He checked his watch. There was still time. The ceremony didn't begin officially for another hour, even though he could already hear murmurs of the gathering crowd outside the chamber's double doors. He pulled out his phone and initiated a call on the frequency specific to vineyard business. No response. He tried calling Tarik's actual cell phone and got voicemail.

Crap. If Sander had arrived—and since Kat had shown up, he probably had—chances were high that the two dukes were too wrapped up in each other to pay attention to anything else. A pang of envy shot through Nico's belly. *Will I ever have that kind of love? That kind of partnership?* He doubted it very seriously.

He scooped Polita out of the crate, despite her sleepy mew of protest, and held her against his chest—more cat fur on his clothing—then glanced wildly at the closed chamber doors. He couldn't barge through the Royals in the antechamber, interrupting their gossip and canapés. He hurried for an unobtrusive door, nearly invisible amid the baroque wainscoting, and slipped into the service corridor, startling a couple of the liveried footmen, who were pushing carts laden with chafing dishes.

"Sorry," he mumbled, and tore off down the hall, his oxfords slapping against the practical gray tile. No marble or heavy carpet in the service corridors—one impeded cart wheels, and the other was too slippery for staff sprinting along to meet the Royals' needs, as Nico was doing himself.

He slowed down to catch his breath before he exited between the suits of armor. Even though staff were expected to be present exactly when the Royals required them, they were never supposed to appear as if they'd had to expend *effort* to do so.

As his heart rate calmed, Polita blinked awake and clambered to his shoulder, mewing as if to order him to get on with it. "Yes, Your Highness," he muttered, and opened the door.

The corridor wasn't empty, a few Royals in court finery sauntering by, chatting desultorily as they peered down their noses at the statues lining the walls. Nico didn't recognize them, but that wasn't unusual. His exposure to the vast roster of North Abarran Royals was limited, since Tarik had little use for most of them and the two of them spent most of their time at the vineyard. This was the first Bonfire Fortnight Nico had ever attended at the Palace, since he usually held down the fort at the vineyard while Tarik was, as he put it, *"fulfilling my fucking family obligations."*

But the reverse was also true. The Royals wouldn't know him from the Mad King, so he was able to stride confidently —but not guiltily, even with a kitten shoulder pad—past them and take the turn that led to the family wing. He hesitated at the junction of the corridor that led to the king's offices in one direction and the stairs to his private quarters in the other. Should he drop Polita off in Corin's office?

The sight of the Minister of Powers heading toward the door made up his mind for him. He darted for the stairs, nodding at the guard who stood at its foot.

The guard, to his credit, didn't blink at the sight of Polita. "Business, sir?"

"His Grace of Arles left the corkscrew for the tasting ceremony in His Majesty's sitting room. I don't suppose His Grace is still inside?

The guard's gaze shifted to a point above Nico's shoulder. "Ah, no. I believe His Grace retired to his own quarters with...His Grace."

Just as I suspected. The poor guard was blushing now. "I understand. I'll just nip upstairs and retrieve it quickly before the ceremony, shall I?"

The guard nodded. "Of course, sir. There's no one upstairs. Please carry on." He stood aside and gestured for Nico to proceed.

His hurried footsteps made no sound on the staircase's plush carpet or in the hallway. The door to the sitting room was slightly ajar. *Good.* He could make sure it was empty before he barged in.

Just in case, though, he knocked softly. "Your Majesty?"

Nobody answered, so Nico pushed the door open and peered inside. *Empty.* However, two teacups sat on the marble table by the fire, so someone had been here lately enough that the staff hadn't had a chance to clear away. Worse, though, was that the corkscrew wasn't where his vision had placed it. The only thing on that marble table was the tea service. *Impossible.* His visions were *never* wrong and always looked forward rather than backward.

He closed his eyes, calling up the image again. A flash of platinum above a beveled marble edge. *Not the table.* He opened his eyes and yes, *there*, on the mantelpiece, next to a framed photograph of the two dukes on their wedding day, accompanied by the king and Princess Katalin, lay the corkscrew.

Nico strode across the room to grab it, Polita disapproving of his speed, apparently, since she dug her claws into his blazer. As he dropped the corkscrew into his pocket, his attention was caught by that photograph.

The two dukes were gazing at each other with such obvious love and longing that Nico flushed like the hapless guard. Princess Katalin wore her habitual cheeky grin, clearly thrilled for her brother's happiness. The king... Nico looked closer. The king was smiling, of course—he always smiled for photographers, and Nico had made a guilty practice of cataloging those smiles, whether obviously political when he appeared with other heads of state or Parliament, or the more intimate ones with his family. But he'd never seen this one before.

It wasn't practiced. It wasn't perfect. It wasn't bland. It was tinged with happiness, of course—it was well known how devoted Tarik and the king were to each other—but it was almost...wistful.

As if he can't imagine the same happiness. Nico huffed a soft laugh. *What do you know? The king and I have something in common.*

A thump followed by a soft curse broke Nico out of his reverie. He glanced around. The room was still empty. Had somebody snuck in? *Someone other than me?* But that was different. He had real business.

The noise came again, emanating from behind a door in the corner. Nico knew it didn't lead to the king's quarters. Those doors lay opposite the fireplace. Somebody was lurking in the closet. Somebody that the guard didn't know about.

An odd protectiveness for the king—who definitely didn't need help from somebody as insignificant as Nico—nevertheless boiled up in his chest. He strode across the room and yanked the door open, revealing a closet stocked with spare linens, a modest selection of office supplies, two extra chairs...

And the king.

CHAPTER FOUR

Nico Pereira, still in those blasted adorable glasses, goggled at Bas from the open closet door. "Y-Your Majesty? If you don't mind my asking—what are you doing in here?"

Bas glanced down at the beribboned decree dangling from his fingers. "It would appear that I'm hiding from my wife."

Nico's brows drew together, creating a far too delectable furrow in his forehead. "Your wife? But, Your Majesty, you're not married. Er…are you?"

Bastien sighed and leaned his head against the spare table linens. "Technically, no." He brandished the document. "But I'm as trapped as if I were."

"Surely… That is, marriage isn't a trap. Or it doesn't have to be. Look at Their Graces."

"Trust me, I'm well aware of the felicity of a marriage of true minds, not to mention hearts. That, I fear, is not to be my fate." He ought to stand up. He had obligations today. The tasting ceremony. *And apparently my engagement announcement.* Bas never shirked his obligations, but that one wasn't something he could face quite yet.

He rolled his head to feast his eyes on Nico again—nobody could arrest him for looking, surely, especially if nobody caught him at it. He squinted up at the man, the overhead lights obviously playing havoc with his vision. "What in blazes is that on your shoulder?"

Nico startled, as if he'd forgotten his passenger was present. "It's a kitten, Your Majesty."

"I'm aware it's a kitten. What is it doing here and why are you wearing it? Has some benighted social influencer declared that felines are this year's must-have fashion accessory?"

Nico's full lips lifted in a smile, and while Bas had been certain that nothing could be more alluring than those glasses, he'd clearly been mistaken. "Of course not. I'm... watching her for Princess Katalin."

"Ah. Say no more." If Helena was a formidable force to be reckoned with, Tarik's new sister-in-law was the equivalent of a category five hurricane.

The kitten tilted her head, returning Bastien's gaze—although technically, he wasn't looking at her, still occupied as he was with cataloging Nico's other enticing features. Then she did something truly alarming—she jumped from Nico's shoulder to Bastien's knee and batted at the ribbons. He reared back, raising the parchment out of her reach and losing his grip on it in the process.

"Oh, I beg your pardon, Your Majesty." Nico, clearly flustered, crouched down to retrieve it. "I'm afraid she has rather strong opinions."

"Well, she is a cat, after all. I've been told that even Katalin has difficulty negotiating with them at times."

"Shall I contact your valet for a clothes brush?" He gestured to his own outfit, which was liberally besmirched with white and orange fur—presumably black as well, but it wasn't visible against the dark cloth. "She has a tendency to shed, I'm afraid."

Bastien waved Nico's worried words away and chucked the kitten under the chin, causing her to close her eyes in bliss and begin a purr that should be bottled, it was so captivatingly perfect. "There's no need." His clothing was never anything less than pristine, and he doubted a tiny kitten would be able to conquer what gravy, wine, and mud hadn't managed.

Nico was still on his haunches, close enough that Bastien could feel his breath stirring the air in the stuffy closet. "Is there something I can do for you, Your Majesty?"

Bastien laughed mirthlessly. "Not unless you can find the loophole in that betrothal contract."

To his surprise, Nico took him seriously. He nodded briskly and stood up, adjusting his glasses—*God*—to read the document.

"Do you always wear glasses?"

Nico started, flushing slightly and blinking at Bas as if he'd said something completely ridiculous. Which, to be fair, he had. First requesting, albeit facetiously, for Nico to peruse the contract, and then following it up with a massive non sequitur. "N-no. But I lost one of my contacts and the replacement hasn't arrived yet."

"Of course. I apologize."

"I took no offense, Your Majesty," he murmured, then returned his focus to the document, leaving Bastien to pet the purring kitten and study Nico out of the corner of his eye. *No hardship there.*

"I take it," Nico said carefully, as if he were afraid of causing offense of his own, "that it's not your wish to wed Lady Helena?"

Bas snorted, hardly a kinglike sound, and the kitten apparently agreed because she dug her claws through his trousers and into his flesh. He gently disengaged them. "Sorry, little one." He glanced up at Nico. "Does she have a name?"

"Her Highness said she calls herself Polita."

"Polita." Bas grinned down at the kitten. "So modest, little pretty one. But I can't argue with the verdict." He looked back at Nico. "To answer your question, no. I do not, nor have I ever wished to do so. The betrothal was a mad"—he winced at the unfortunate word choice—"notion on our fathers' part. I could have sworn that Lady Helena was equally averse to the match, but apparently..." He shrugged.

"Ah. Yes. Position and influence. And as I understand it, Royals of your rank are accustomed to marriages of state."

Bastien sighed and scratched Polita behind her ears. "Is it wrong of me to want something more? To wish to make my own choice? To hope for the kind of connection that Tarik has, that my brother has?"

Nico's smile was soft. "No, Your Majesty. I don't think it's wrong at all. I think everyone deserves happiness. Even kings." Polita mewed. "Even disobedient cats."

Bastien inclined his head. "Thank you. However, I fear the die has been cast. I had hoped to find a way to circumvent this, but with Parliament in recess and not reconvening until after the deadline on my birthday—"

"Pardon me, Your Majesty, but if you're not inclined to marry Lady Helena, why not choose your own fiancée?"

Bastien lifted his eyebrows. "Because the choice was taken from me when I was seven years old." Tarik always claimed that Nico was so clever, yet he couldn't interpret a Parliamentary decree? Granted, the language in those blasted things could be convoluted, but the aim was clear.

Nico bit his lip as he frowned down at the parchment. "But I don't think it was. I mean, yes, it was obvious that was the *intent* of the decree, but laws aren't enforced by intent. They're enforced by their precise language. If you take each clause independently, as a barrister would in court, then the last section—"

Hope flared in Bastien's chest. "Give me that." He all but snatched the document out of Nico's hand. "What do you mean?"

"Right here." He touched a paragraph directly above the seal. "It says you must be engaged by sundown on your thirty-third birthday. But that particular clause doesn't specify whom you must be engaged *to*."

The words danced in front of Bastien's eyes as he tried to decipher the formal calligraphy that Parliament still insisted on using for decrees of this nature. *I'm introducing a Royal order—Times New Roman, 12 point, for all official documents from now on.* "Are you positive?"

"I've had some experience with contract law as part of my duties at the vineyard, and I believe that a clever barrister—which I assume you have at your disposal— could make a very solid case. While Lady Helena is mentioned by name here"—he pointed—"and here, her name is not mentioned in the final clause. Furthermore, it appears that as long as the engagement takes place by the deadline, the subsequent wedding is not specifically required."

"*What?*" Bastien read and re-read the final paragraph. "Bloody hell, you're right." The document said: "*Provided Bastien Gauthier Lavigne D'Aramitz is officially engaged to be married by sundown on his thirty-third birthday, the terms of this contract will be exercised in full.*"

"You see? It only says *you* need to be engaged, not Lady Helena. And the engagement terminates the contract." He shrugged diffidently. "I expect that's because in the days when this contract was drawn up, breaking a royal engagement was simply not done."

"Thank goodness for ne'er-do-well Royals who set unfortunate selfish precedents," Bas murmured like a prayer.

"There's only one slight problem, Your Majesty," Nico said apologetically.

Since he felt as if the weight of Mount Abarra had been lifted off his shoulders, Bas was almost giddy, joy and relief welling up inside him, warm and effervescent. At this point, he could brave even the Minister of Powers and inform him, oh so haughtily, that the Calibration Ceremony would have to wait until after his wedding, which he could put off indefinitely.

"Whatever it is, I'm sure Vidal can handle it. He handles everything."

"I, um, don't think he can handle this, Your Majesty."

Bas grinned up at Nico. God, he looked positively edible with that worried frown pleating his forehead above those enchanting glasses. "Nonsense. He's omnipotent. Rather like Tarik considers you, as a matter of fact." He held Polita up in front of his face and touched her nose with his. "Isn't that right, pretty one?"

"Your Majesty, please." Nico's tone was almost desperate. "I'm sorry to contradict you, but you must listen."

He settled Polita against his chest, where she batted at one of his medals. "Very well. I'm listening. But I fail to see how anything you say can dampen my elation at avoiding an engagement to Helena Rey."

"But that's just it. You can't."

Bas frowned, his grip tightening on Polita's silky fur, much to her apparent displeasure, since she let out a tiny hiss. "You said I could."

"You can avoid engagement to Lady Helena—*if* you're engaged to somebody else." Nico spread his hands, palms up. "You have to find a fiancée by next Thursday at sundown."

Bas's mood tumbled into the crapper. *Blast.* It wasn't as if he had a dozen possibilities. His obligations as king made any kind of relationship difficult, if not impossible. Polita wriggled in his grasp. *Katalin.* She was his closest friend outside Tarik, Sander, and, sad as it seemed, his personal secretary. But an engagement to a South Abarran princess would cause complications for both of them—and require an act of Parliament from both countries, given how agitated both governments had gotten over Tarik wedding Sander. Such an engagement would be impossible to subsequently escape, and he couldn't foist that onto Kat. He knew for a fact she didn't want a state marriage any more than he did.

He frowned, scratching under Polita's chin as he met Nico's worried gaze. *Those glasses. They just kill me.*

Wait. "So, Nico…"

"Yes, Your Majesty?"

"You asked whether there was anything you could do for me. Did you mean it?"

"Of course. I'd do anything for you, just as I would for His Grace."

"Excellent." Bastien grinned and slid off the chair to drop to one knee, holding up the decree like an offering. "Marry me."

For an instant, as the king sank so gracefully in front of him, Nico's heart fluttered like a captive dove. "Wh-what?" Reflexively, he took the contract from the king's hand.

But then the king rose again, Polita still cradled against his chest. "Obviously we wouldn't actually get married. We only need to announce our engagement and maintain the ruse until after my birthday." His brows drew together. "Well, after Bonfire Fortnight. Yes, that would be better. We need to remain believably attached for as long as the Reys are here."

Of course. This had nothing to do with any feelings the king had for Nico. Hell, Nico was surprised the king even knew his name. "So, what you're saying is that you want me to be your future ex-fiancé?"

The king's brow cleared and he beamed. "Exactly! Once Parliament has verified contract fulfillment, we can quietly break the engagement and everything can go back to normal."

Nico dropped his gaze to his feet, the last of his thrill thoroughly quenched. "I see." The king didn't want *him*. He just needed a fake fiancé and Nico happened to be the first unattached person to step into the closet.

Wait. The closet.

"Your Majesty, will your engagement to a man be credible? Accepted?"

The king waved one hand, the one with the heavy royal signet. "It's common knowledge that I'm pan. It won't be an issue."

Nico suddenly realized that he was mere inches from the king, that the height difference between them—the king only an inch or so taller—made their lips a most convenient kissing distance. "Oh," he breathed.

The king raised an eyebrow. "So perhaps we should leave the closet both literally and figuratively?"

Nico startled. "Yes. Of course. I'm sorry, Your Majesty." He backed out of the closet, his heel catching on the threshold and nearly sending him onto his ass. Only the king's hand on his arm kept him on his feet.

The king's low chuckle did unfortunate things to Nico's middle. "Under the circumstances, perhaps you should call me Bastien."

Nico's eyes widened. "I— I couldn't."

"I expect you could if you tried." He winked—the king actually *winked*. "After all, you did say you'd do anything for me."

Nico narrowed his eyes. "You're going to hold that over me forever, aren't you?" However, that is what he'd said, and he always kept his word.

The king—*Bastien*—looked immediately contrite. "I beg your pardon. I have no desire to coerce you in any way. I'm not my father. I'm not the Mad King—although when Tarik gets wind of this scheme, he may beg to differ," he muttered.

"If you don't mind my saying so, I don't think telling His Grace that the engagement is a sham would be the best strategy." Although his head was spinning slightly at the unreality of this situation—the king had *proposed* to him!— Nico's problem-solving training kicked in. "In order to make this believable, we can't let anyone else know that it's not real."

Bastien's dark brown eyes lit up. "You mean you'll do it? I understand being the king's fiancé—and then the king's ex —could present a certain amount of inconvenience."

Nico smiled wanly. "I'm staff, Your Maj—Bastien. Our inconvenience in the service of the Royals is kind of SOP."

Bastien winced. "Ah. I suppose that's true. We Royals are a spoiled and privileged lot, through nothing more than an accident of birth."

Guilt squirmed in Nico's middle. "No! I didn't mean— That is, I think you're a good king. A wonderful king, and a good man. But that doesn't negate the fact that there's a very wide social gap between us."

"And a definite power imbalance," Bastien murmured. "Yes, I see how that notion might be difficult for some to overcome. Tarik and Sander faced significant opposition, and their relative rank within our countries was, for all intents and purposes, identical." He strolled over to the wingback chair by the fireplace and sank down on it, settling Polita on his lap. He cast a decidedly mischievous smile at Nico. "On the other hand, you're the only North Abarran in history to receive the Mixtel Cross for distinguished service to the South Abarran crown, so you have a bit of a pedigree of your own."

"I'm a commoner, Your— Bastien. And you're putting a great deal of trust in someone who, if you'll pardon me for saying so, you know very little about."

Bastien rested his hands on Polita's back. "I know that you moved heaven and earth—hell, you moved the governments of two fractious countries—to rescue my best friend. I know that Tarik trusts you with more than his life —he trusts you with *Sander's* life, which is far more precious to him. I know that Princess Katalin, who is one of the shrewdest judges of character I've ever met, thinks highly enough of you to entrust this little one"—he stroked Polita's forehead with one finger—"to you, and when it comes to animals, Kat *never* takes chances."

Heat rushed up Nico's throat at the praise, and from how warm his cheeks felt, he was probably blushing hotly enough to be seen from space. "Th-thank you for the compliments, Y— Bastien."

"See? You're getting used to it already. You barely had to catch yourself that time." He gestured to the chair opposite him. "Please. Sit."

Nico swallowed but followed instructions, under no illusion that the request was optional. But as he sank into the chair, something sharp poked his hip. *The corkscrew.* He jumped up again. "The tasting ceremony! We don't have time—"

"Nonsense." Bastien gestured for him to resume his seat. "They can hardly start without me, can they? And I'm sure Tarik and Sander won't object to a bit more privacy before facing the crowd, many of whom are still somewhat rankled by their marriage."

"That's exactly what I mean. If people objected to their marriage, what do you imagine they'll think about the king —the *king*—getting engaged to a commoner?"

"They'll probably say any number of things. Think any number of things. *Shout* any number of things." He leaned forward. "I'm used to that, Nico. Every time I leave the Palace, I'm sure to pass at least one or two protests, signs calling me *King Bastard*. How many of my subjects do you suppose will be tossing effigies of *me* onto the fire on Bonfire Night, rather than the traditional Louis IV poppets? I know for a fact there are shops in North Dulibre that sell them."

There were. Nico had seen them and been outraged on Bastien's behalf. "This could make things worse."

"On the contrary, it might make things better." Bastien leaned back in the chair, absently petting Polita, an arrested expression on his face. "Many of the protests are about the inequities between Royals and commoners. Perhaps this engagement might somewhat mollify those factions who are most militant."

"Then what do you think will happen when you break the engagement?"

"We'll worry about that later."

"No. I think we need to worry about it now. Both of us are risking a lot if we do this. For all you know, I could blackmail you. Force you to marry me under threat of publicizing your efforts to circumvent Parliament and contract law."

"And for all you know, I could only be promising you power and riches just so I could lure you into my bed."

Nico's mouth dried. "Uh…"

"Relax, Nico. I wouldn't dream of using our agreement as a way to pressure you into having sex with me. As I said, I'm not my father and I'm not the Mad King."

Nico glanced at the sealed and beribboned document that he still held clutched in his hand, his grip wrinkling the thick parchment. "Perhaps, since we're attempting to circumvent a contract, we should have one of our own. One that spells out expectations. Non-disclosure. Exit strategy."

Bastien inclined his head. "If that's what you wish. You are doing me an immense favor, Nico, after already doing an even larger one by pointing out the loophole in that blasted betrothal contract. Draw up whatever you wish and we'll sign copies for each of us. Then stow them in safe places." He grinned crookedly. "We can have our own private bonfire when we terminate the engagement and burn them in this very fireplace, if you like."

Nico nodded jerkily. "I'd prefer that. Keeping this professional." Heat infused his face again. "Not that I'm a— Not that there's anything *wrong* with that kind of— I mean, I don't make it a habit to—"

"Hire yourself out as arm candy to needy Royals?" Bastien said dryly.

Nico was surprised into a laugh. "I couldn't be arm candy to anybody."

"That's where you're wrong," Bastien murmured.

At least, that's what Nico *thought* he said, but he must have been mistaken. *What am I doing?* Was he really considering becoming the king's fiancé? The king's *fake* fiancé? The fallout from this would be— Nico didn't want to think about it. Bastien would probably survive it—he had resources that could weather almost any storm. *Other than being forced into a state marriage, apparently.* But Nico had nothing—just his job and his reputation. Could he come out the other side of this agreement with both of those intact?

"You seem…hesitant, Nico," Bas said softly. "Are you having second thoughts? I'm perfectly willing to include suitable remuneration for—"

"No! The last thing I want from you is money. That's not why I'm doing this." A vision materialized in his mind's eye: a contract—single page, his signature and Bastien's affixed to the bottom—being locked inside a safe. *Well. I guess I really am doing this.*

Bastien inclined his head. "As you wish."

"It'll take me a couple of hours to put the agreement together."

"But you've already said that we don't have that much time." He shrugged, and even that was graceful. Polita scrambled from his lap to his shoulder—and really, why wasn't that forest green jacket covered in cat fur and pulled threads? "A few minutes' delay of the tasting ceremony might be acceptable. Two hours might be construed as a comment about the first joint venture between North and South." He grinned. "Well, the first other than your successful campaign to rescue the two dukes and facilitate their subsequent marriage, of course. But I can't appear less than 100% in favor of these new efforts."

"Of course not. But—"

Bastien stood, transferring Polita from his shoulder to the chair cushion, where, surprisingly enough, she curled up and closed her eyes. "I trust you, Nico. You're saving me from a fate I thought inevitable, and I won't let you suffer for that." He held out his hand, as if to shake. "Make a few notes, and we'll settle the remaining details after the ceremony."

Nico took Bastien's hand. It was warm, the palm unexpectedly roughened by a ridge of calluses below the fingers. "Agreed."

Bastien's grip tightened. "Although I should warn you— the announcement will probably take place at the tasting ceremony, since that's when my mother and apparently Lady Helena were expecting it to occur. Are you ready?"

Other than having a belly full of snakes, a jacket covered with cat fur, and an unrequited crush? "Absolutely."

CHAPTER FIVE

Despite the shoulder-to-shoulder crowd in the audience chamber, Bas wasn't overheated, because of course he wasn't. But Tarik, who hadn't strayed more than two steps from Sander since Bas had joined them here on the dais, backed by a veritable wall of wine cases, pulled irritably at his collar.

"Why the fuck do you keep the Palace so hot?"

Bas maintained his mildly pleased expression, the one he used in the lead-up to positive PR appearances, although his gaze kept flicking to Nico, who was standing next to the dais, that same worry pleat between his brows. "The temperature is maintained at sixty-five Fahrenheit in the winter and seventy-five in the summer."

"Well, clearly it needs adjusting for fucking springtime, because—"

"Tarik," Bas murmured, pleased that his voice didn't wobble given the butterflies gyrating in his midsection, "I suggest you keep your more colorful language locked down a trifle, considering the room is filled to its distant rafters with Royals, members of Parliament—"

"If they don't know me by now—"

"Not to mention members of the press. Think of Sander."

Tarik shot him a glare from under his brows. "Low blow, Bas."

"Whatever works," Bas replied blandly.

But as Bas scanned the crowd, he could readily understand why the palace's environmental controls were having difficulty. Counteracting the heat thrown out by so many overdressed bodies was a challenge for any HVAC system, even one as high-end as theirs.

Several rows of chairs were lined up directly in front of the dais for the higher-ranked Royals or those who weren't able to stand for extended periods. His mother was sitting in the center of the first row, smiling delightedly up at him. He doubted very seriously whether her delight had anything to do with a wine tasting, regardless of the symbolic nature of this particular vintage.

She's anticipating my engagement announcement.

In fact, Helena was sitting on Genevieve's immediate right, and Genevieve held Helena's hand as if the two of them were contestants on that British baking show, waiting to hear who would be voted out of the tent.

Newsflash: It's you, Helena.

Would she be relieved to be free of the shackles of an agreement she hadn't chosen anymore than Bas had? They'd been children who hadn't even liked one another. On the other hand, he was about to eliminate her opportunity to ascend to a rank and power that nearly matched his own. Would she thank him for stripping that prize from her, assuming she even considered it a prize?

He glanced at Nico again, guilt twisting like taffy in his belly. *What am I asking of him? Is it fair? Am I using him to get what I want?*

Well, obviously the answer to that was yes. But Nico knew the terms, had agreed to them, had negotiated a few of his own. Bas had offered him a fountain pen and the back of the decree to make notes, but Nico had looked positively scandalized and unearthed a stray packing list from the closet to sketch the bones of their agreement. They'd initialed it for now, pending the final version later, but Nico would be protected. He wasn't trapped in this forever, and nor was Bas.

The taffy twisted tighter as Nico handed the commemorative platinum corkscrew to Tarik. It would be preserved in the National Museum as a symbol of the new age of cooperation between North and South Abarra. Would being the king's ex make Nico another curio in that museum exhibit? Or would he be able to return to his normal life once this...this...

He covered a laugh by pretending to cough. Katalin would call *this* a dog-and-pony show, but to Bas, it was more like an illusionist's trick. Once his birthday was past, the contract broken, Nico could step into the vanishing cabinet and disappear without so much as a *hey, presto!*

But could he? That was the question. Would he be dogged by paparazzi while he tried to do his job at the vineyard, pressured to pen a tell-all book with real or imagined slights perpetrated by the king who had jilted him, or targeted by the same factions that had threatened Sander and Tarik?

No. One way or another, Bas wouldn't let that happen. Nico wouldn't suffer because of his generosity of spirit, his willingness to help—hell, from his brilliant solution for rescuing Bas from his chains.

Opposite Nico, on the other side of the dais, Gaston stood like a brick wall, his hands clasped behind his back, earpiece in place, no doubt monitoring check-ins from his team stationed throughout the room. From the way Tarik's gaze flicked from one spot to another, he was monitoring their message frequency, which was probably the only reason he wasn't tucked under Sander's arm.

Bas glanced at Nico again. No guards stood near him. *That needs to change.* Did he realize it? Tarik complained about the need for guards all the time and he was used to it.

God, I should have thought this through more. Bas was gaining everything. Nico was gaining nothing, and in fact could be sacrificing more than he knew. Maybe it wasn't too late—

"Honored guests," Baroness Savatier announced through her mic, the echo muted by the mass of bodies in the room, "King Bastien Gauthier Lavigne D'Aramitz, Prime Minister the right honorable Lady Isabel Beaufort, and the members of the North Abarran Parliament welcome you to the inaugural event of this year's Bonfire Fortnight. I give you His Royal Highness Tarik Jaso, Duke of Arles."

It was definitely too late.

Somehow Bas kept his PR-pleasant smile in place as Tarik described the historic joint effort on behalf of North and South Abarran winemaking. Under cover of acknowledging the occasional applause, Bas monitored Nico, who was looking decidedly nervous and rather adorably rumpled, his charcoal blazer speckled with cat fur; and Helena, who was looking…what? Resigned? Determined? Smug? He couldn't tell. Every time he glanced her way, he had to look away quickly lest he catch her eye.

Blast. I should have warned her. But it was also too late for that.

Tarik drew the cork from the specially labeled wine with a pop and passed the bottle to his husband, who poured a sample into the crystal glass etched with the D'Aramitz crest. "Your Majesty, would you care to taste Royal Roses Red?"

Bas inclined his head and accepted the wine from Sander. "I would be honored, Your Grace."

He took his time, swirling the wine in the glass, letting its fruity aroma develop and deepen. He took a sip, let it roll on his tongue. The flavor was full-bodied, complex, satisfying. Notes of vanilla, plum, chocolate, and of course, oak from Sander's hand-crafted aging barrels.

He opened his eyes and lifted his glass. "A triumph, Your Graces. It will be my honor to serve it at the state dinner next week on Bonfire Night. Although I confess I'll reserve several cases for my own personal table." He smiled out at the audience as Sander filled the other two glasses and added more to Bas's. The three of them raised their arms in a toast. "To the first of many fruitful partnerships between North and South Abarra."

The three of them drank as the audience—far too exalted for anything as plebeian as a cheer—clapped politely.

"Psst."

Bastien glanced around at the hiss, wondering if Polita had managed to escape his sitting room. But it was his mother, leaning forward in her chair. *Oh dear.* If she was having one of her episodes, this could get awkward very quickly.

He smiled down at her. "What is it, Mother?"

"Don't you have…something else to announce?"

"Yes, of course." Bas held up his glass and smiled blandly at the crowd. "If any of you would like a case of this excellent wine for your own cellars, Their Graces have thoughtfully brought a supply with them." He turned to Tarik. "Your Grace? How might our esteemed guests claim a case for their own?"

"By donating to the New Abarran Animal Rescue League, a worthy cause that's already making a difference across North Abarra."

"…Southern plot."

Bas couldn't identify the mutter, but Gaston's eyes had narrowed, and he murmured instructions to his team, so they were on it. Bas caught Tarik's movement out of the corner of his eye as he took Sander's hand.

Tarik stared, steely eyed, at the crowd. "My assistant will assist you with—"

"No!"

Tarik gaped at Bas's outburst, and he wasn't alone. Most of the audience was blinking at him too. He never raised his voice in these kinds of events. But he couldn't let Nico be inundated by Royals clamoring to claim cases of wine in an attempt to curry favor. *Blast.* This arrangement would affect Tarik too. *I really should have thought this through more.*

But the only way around was through. Bas smiled benignly. "I have another announcement to make, one that perhaps many of you have expected for several years." He lifted his eyebrow with the rueful smile he was aware conveyed the perfect blend of contrition and authority. "Particularly considering my advancing years."

The crowd laughed in response, as was intended. His mother sat forward, her eyes sparkling. *She's going to be disappointed.* He should have given her advance warning too, except she'd have been just as likely to forget.

He raised his chin, his gaze focused above the heads of the crowd so he wouldn't meet anyone's eyes. "Today, I'm pleased and humbled to announce that I am at last engaged to be married." The crowd gasped, his mother clapped, and Helena shifted in her seat as if she were about to stand up. "May I present to you my fiancé?" Helena half-rose, but Bas turned to hold out a hand to Nico. "Nico Pereira."

This time, the crowd's gasp wasn't feigned, an angry murmur growing like a wave about to crash. Helena sank back into her chair, her expression one of shock. His mother simply looked confused.

She glanced between him and Helena. "But—"

"Nico, please join me, my dear?" Bas beckoned, since Nico appeared to have been turned to stone. Bas glanced at Gaston. "Gaston, if you would be so kind?"

Gaston nodded to his second in command, Pascal, who strode to Nico's side and escorted him the two steps to the dais.

Nico stumbled a little on the first step, but Pascal steadied him with a hand on his elbow as Tarik growled, "What the actual fuck, Bas?"

"Later, Tarik." Bas murmured. "Please."

To Tarik's credit, he complied, clapping Nico on the shoulder as he passed to take his place at Bas's side.

"Honored guests, you may remember Nico as the sole Northern recipient of the Mixtel Cross for his devotion and tireless efforts in rescuing Their Graces two years ago. Since that time, I've come to know him better, and I believe that once you get to know him too, you'll love him as much as I do."

Love. Nico swallowed hard as Bas took his hand with the eyes of the entire North Abarran Royal contingent boring into them. Love wasn't on the agenda. In fact, this whole arrangement was the opposite of love. *And I clearly didn't appreciate exactly what it would mean.*

Because as he stood at Bas's side, members of the press shouting questions and straining to get past the king's guards, Bas's mother and actual ex goggling at them from the front row, it finally hit him that this wasn't as simple as helping the king out of an unwanted betrothal contract. It wasn't like changing labeling vendors or installing a new fermentation tank.

This was a big fricking deal.

He shot a panicked glance at Tarik, who was clutching Sander's hand, his mouth set in a grim line. *Does he blame me? Does he think I'm as unworthy as I feel? God, will anybody even* believe *this?*

His gaze snagged on Bastien's mother, Queen Genevieve, sitting bewildered in the first row, and his heart seemed to freeze in his chest. At Sander and Tarik's pre-wedding reception, he'd overheard a conversation between the

Queen Mum, Tarik, and Bastien. When Tarik had tried to delay departure for the traditional march through the North Abarran streets to the celebratory wedding eve meal, Queen Genevieve had declared that Nico *wasn't family*. He'd been excluded from the dinner he'd helped to plan, and that was for her nephew, not her only son.

God, what would she think of this?

Lady Helena, too. Even if she was as opposed or at least indifferent to the match as Bas claimed that he was, this had to come as a shock. How many people in this room knew about the betrothal? Judging by all the sidelong glances and sly grins being tossed Lady Helena's way, probably everybody. Even if she didn't want the match, having it sprung on her like this must be humiliating. It would be for Nico, if it happened to him.

It will happen to me. In fact, it was already on the calendar. But at least he knew it was coming. Lady Helena had been completely blindsided. Sure enough, her usual perfect appearance was marred by an expression Nico could only describe as sour.

Someone appeared in front of the dais. *Lady Isabel Beaufort. The Prime Minister.* Accompanied by Baroness Savatier, the Crown's Chamberlain, who was even more intimidating.

"Your Majesty," Lady Isabel said, "we need to talk."

"It's Bonfire Fortnight, Prime Minister." Bastien smiled benignly. "I'm sure whatever you'd like to discuss can wait until Parliament reconvenes."

"No," she said grimly. "It cannot."

Bastien gripped Nico's hand a little tighter. "Very well. Nico will accompany us—"

"No. He cannot." Lady Isabel grimaced. "I beg your pardon, Your Majesty, but this is a private matter between the Crown and the government."

"In any case," Baroness Savatier said in her rather gruff voice, "I require Mr. Pereira's presence."

Nico's gaze flew to Bastien's face, and no doubt he looked as panicked as he felt. Bastien placed Nico's hand on his arm, the wool of Bastien's uniform smooth under his palm, and covered it with his own. "I'd prefer to be present during any interview you might require for Nico."

Thank goodness. Nico had confidence in his ability to handle most situations, but he'd never been called upon to play the role of sudden royal fiancé. Maybe he could hide in Tarik's office until Bastien was free. They still needed to finalize their own private contract. Make it more formal than scribbled notes on the back of an office supply invoice.

But Baroness Savatier shook her head, her cap of gray curls not daring to bounce. "You needn't fear for his safety, Your Majesty. As a matter of fact, my intention is to secure it." She nodded at the guard who had appeared next to the dais after the announcement. "Gaston has assigned Pascal as Mr. Pereira's personal guard for the moment. I've arranged temporary quarters for him. We're merely escorting him there now so he can settle in and await your return."

A personal guard? Quarters? Nico had never had either before. If he had to stay overnight in the Palace, he usually stayed in Tarik's quarters, although that wasn't possible with Sander in residence. Nico had a room reserved at a modest inn in the city, near the Palace grounds, for the duration of Bonfire Fortnight. *I suppose I should cancel the reservation.* And as for guards, usually he spent his time either dodging them or presenting them with the clearance codes necessary for him to infiltrate the private areas of the Palace.

Ugh. Infiltrate. That made him sound like what he was— an unwanted interloper, like the cockroaches that had invaded Isola Alessi and derailed Tarik's wedding plans.

From the way most of the Royals in the audience were glowering at him, their lips lifted in disgust, they probably ranked him on a par with cockroaches, or perhaps several rungs lower.

"We'll accompany Nico," Tarik growled, and from the way Sander was wincing, Tarik's grip on his hand wasn't precisely gentle.

"I'm sorry, Your Grace," Baroness Savatier said, not sounding at all sorry, "but you don't have appropriate clearance for the royal suitor's quarters."

"What?" Tarik's scowl would have sent a lesser woman than Baroness Savatier scampering for the hills. "But—"

"Tarik," Bastien said evenly, "perhaps we should allow the Baroness to do her job."

Tarik frowned at Bastien, but nodded curtly. "Fine." Sander gave Nico a reassuring, albeit strained, smile.

"Of course, Baroness. Thank you." Nico released Bastien's arm, but Bastien caught his hand and drew him forward to kiss his cheek.

"Until later, my dear."

Nico could only blink stupidly for a moment, his cheek tingling from the press of Bastien's lips. Then Baroness Savatier cleared her throat.

"This way, Mr. Pereira."

Nico stumbled off the dais and was immediately flanked by the ramrod-straight Baroness and the hulking Pascal, who probably could make two of Nico with some left over.

She didn't bother to clear a path through the Royals, who were still milling about, muttering under their breaths. Nico half expected random fights to break out, as if they were a barely contained pack of wild dogs.

Pascal opened the door at the back of the chamber, one that Nico had never noticed before, so well camouflaged was it. It led not to the service corridors he was familiar with, but to what had to be a private passage reserved for

Royals. They wouldn't waste carpeting this lush, not to mention paintings that ought to be hanging in the National Museum, on a hallway used only by staff.

Despite the nerves playing marbles in his belly, Nico studied their route carefully, trying to envision where it fell in relation to the other access corridors. *With all these stairs and hallways, I'm surprised they managed to squeeze in any actual rooms.*

They emerged in the same hallway as the king's—as *Bastien*'s—private quarters, and Nico swallowed thickly. *I'm going to live in the same place as the king.* His mother, were she still living, would never believe it.

The Baroness flicked a finger at a door across the hallway from Bastien's sitting room, and Pascal sprang forward— pretty spryly for such a big man—opened the door, and then stood aside to allow Nico and the Baroness to enter.

The room was a mirror of Bastien's room, from the fireplace and its flanking chairs, the marble-topped table between them, the desk and worktable, the—Nico gulped— closet in the corner. No less luxurious, no less well- appointed. *A room fit for a King.* Definitely not fit for an impostor.

But the thing that truly made Nico's jaw drop was Corin, standing at attention in front of the desk, his tablet in the crook of his arm, and a glint in his eye that promised Nico would be enduring the third degree from his friend in the not-too-distant future. *Not that I can tell him anything. I promised.*

The Baroness turned to Nico. "I believe you know Mr. Vidal. He'll act as your personal secretary until you're able to hire one of your own."

"P-personal secretary?" Nico licked his dry lips. "Do I need a personal secretary?"

"Certainly," the Baroness said, her severe tone somewhat softened by the lift of one graying eyebrow. "The Royal

Consort has nearly as many obligations as the king. You'll have an entire staff at your disposal, but I'll need some time to vet the best candidates for you to interview."

"Interview?" Nico said faintly.

"For the moment, please make yourself comfortable. You have a dressing room through there"—she pointed to a door opposite the fireplace—"a bathroom"—another door—"and a bedroom beyond for your use until you and the king are wed when you will move into his quarters. We'll have your belongings transferred as soon as possible if you'd tell us where..." She let her voice lift in a delicate inquiry.

"Um..."

"No worries, Baroness," Corin said brightly. "I've already dispatched a footman to collect them from the inn."

"Inn?" Her voice dipped as if Corin had announced that Nico had been residing in a leper colony.

Corin grinned, perhaps a little too widely. "Perfectly respectable, I assure you."

The Baroness was not charmed. "But the king's fiancé should not be staying at an unsecured location."

"Now he's not." Corin inclined his head. "You needn't worry, Baroness. I have everything in hand."

She narrowed her eyes at him, but returned his bow. "Very well." She turned to Nico. "If you require anything, Mr. Pereira, you need only to mention it to Pascal, or to call 9-7 on the house phone." She indicated a multi-line phone on the desk. Seriously? He needed a multi-line phone *and* a personal secretary? "We look forward to serving you."

She bowed again—to Nico this time—and glided out of the room on her sensible shoes.

Nico almost wished for her to come back, because now he had to face his friend. He turned slowly, a sickly smile pasted on his face. Just as he suspected, Corin was giving him a basilisk stare.

"So." Nico laughed weakly. "Personal secretary?"

"If I imagined for *one stinking second* that you and the king had been carrying on a star-crossed love affair under my nose, I'd...I'd..." He huffed. "Well, I'm not sure what I would do."

"Um..."

"But luckily for you..." He prowled toward Nico until they were practically nose to nose. "I found this." He flipped open the cover on his tablet and extracted a rather grubby piece of paper that Nico recognized all too well.

My notes. He slapped ineffectually at his obviously empty pockets. How had he forgotten to take those with him? But they'd been left in Bastien's sitting room. *Which...Corin has access to.*

"Look. Corin. I can explain. I—mmmph." Nicos face was suddenly mooshed against Corin's chest.

"I can't believe you found a way to save him. *Thank you.*" He stepped away, but gripped Nico's shoulders, his eyes shiny with unshed tears. "I've been *agonizing* about this ever since I took this job."

"You...you mean you don't mind?"

"Mind? Are you kidding? This is *brilliant.*" He let go of Nico's shoulders and poked him in the chest. "But you and the king need some serious instruction on how to keep things under wraps. What the hell? You left these notes where anybody could find them."

"I thought I'd put them in my pocket. I was...distracted." *By Bastien's eyes.* And shoulders. And everything else.

Corin smirked. "I'll wager you were. Living a little teenaged dream, are you? After all, you had that poster of him hanging over your bed. Framed."

"That was a collectible! An original from his coronation. It's not like he was some shirtless romance cover model."

"You sighed over it as though he was."

"Shut up," Nico said sulkily.

Corin laughed. "You're so easy. And damn lucky that *I* was the one who found your incriminating notes. I've taken the liberty of finalizing the contract. It's ready for both of you to sign."

"You did?" Nico heaved a sigh of relief. "*Thank* you. Lady Isabel towed Bastien away before we—"

"Hold it." Corin clutched Nico's arm. "Lady Isabel? Was the Minister of Powers there too?"

Nico bit his lip. "Maybe? I try to avoid looking at him whenever I can."

"Don't we all," Corin muttered. He crossed to the fireplace and tossed the notes into the flames, using a poker to make sure they were burned to ash and the ashes scattered. "Now, come on. We need to go rescue your fake fiancé."

CHAPTER SIX

Lady Isabel, as was her habit, was powering down the corridor toward her Palace offices as if the carpet had somehow offended her. Since she was about a foot shorter than Bas, he had no trouble keeping up, even though he kept his stride even and unhurried.

He'd long ago mastered the ability to assess his surroundings surreptitiously, so he took mental notes of the expressions on the faces of Royals and staff as they passed. *Angry. Stunned. Gleeful. Relieved. Bored.* The whole gamut, but from what he could tell, no particular reaction had the majority yet. Isabel hadn't picked up any other people along the way for their little tête-à-tête, thank goodness—people like the Minister of Powers, or Lady Helena, or worse: his mother.

They passed through Lady Isabel's antechamber, her secretary staring at them wide-eyed from behind her desk, and Gaston hurried ahead to open the door to her inner office and allow them to enter. "I'll be outside, Your Majesty."

"Thank you, Gaston." He turned to Isabel as the door clicked shut behind him. "Well?"

She glared at him. Then shook her head and said, "For God's sake, Your Majesty. What have you done to us?"

"'Us?' I wasn't aware that my marriage comprised more than my future husband and myself."

She pointed a blunt finger at him, its nail unpolished but neatly trimmed. "Don't be glib. You know perfectly well what I mean. Every single member of Parliament was expecting Lady Helena Rey to be the Queen Consort by this time next year. They'd already started jockeying for favor with her father, much to his evident glee. You've just disrupted the power balance that's been months—no, *years* in the making."

"Maybe disrupting the power balance is good for the country." Bas strolled over and dropped into the brocade armchair that was reserved for his use here, more so that she could sit than that he wanted to himself. He'd much prefer to pace off his residual adrenaline. "The existing power balance has trapped us in decades—no, *centuries* of archaic traditions," he said, deliberately matching her cadence. "You're a progressive, Isabel. Surely you agree with me."

She sank down in the chair behind her desk, a chair that was sized for a much larger person. *I should arrange more appropriate seating for her.* "Whether I agree with you or not, upsetting the cart this way isn't beneficial for anyone—you, me, or the country."

"I'm not certain how sacrificing both myself and Lady Helena on the altar of our fathers' mutual machinations would help anybody."

She lifted an eyebrow. "It would help Lady Helena. And it would most certainly help her family and their political aspirations."

"All the more reason to avoid the match." Bas had heard more than he ever wanted to about Ferran Rey's mining agenda. He'd thought the duke had retreated somewhat, since he was getting a lot of traction out of Sander Fiala's magnetism experiments. But the promise of power was its own seductive sinkhole.

"Your Majesty." She sighed, and for an instant, the harsh sunlight striking in through the window illuminated the lines on her face in a way that made her look...old. "He's a *commoner*."

"That will be remedied as soon as he marries me. We should probably discuss his titles now. Or can that wait until Parliament reconvenes?"

"He's a commoner *and a man*. One of the reasons Parliament has left you relatively alone is because they saw the betrothal contract as insurance. A promise that you'd be wed at a reasonable age and that an heir would be forthcoming to secure the succession."

"That's irrelevant, and you know it. North Abarra has the most progressive surrogacy regulations in all of Europe, perhaps the world. I could put matters in motion for my heir before the ink is dry on the marriage license."

She squinted at him. "So why haven't you started the process already?"

Fair question. "Because I wanted the pregnancy to be a time of joy and anticipation for me and my spouse, of course. I wouldn't wish to leave them out of it."

She sighed again. "You realize a large swath of Parliament won't accept this new betrothal. They considered the former contract ironclad."

"It's not. The final clause only specifies that I be engaged by my thirty-third birthday. Not to whom."

"It was implicit in the rest of the language—"

"Isabel, you were the most cutthroat solicitor in Perpignan before you went into politics. You know perfectly well that *implicit* won't hold up in court. I have the right to choose my own spouse. My father did not. Nor does Ferran Rey. Nor Parliament."

"You're overreaching yourself, Your Majesty. Parliament does in fact have a say."

"Only the right of refusal. They can block my choice, but they can't pick another one for me."

She gazed at him solemnly. "You should be prepared for a fight. Because there'll be a lot of MPs who'll climb on that bandwagon."

He smiled at her blandly. "I trust that you and the progressives will be able to negotiate a reasonable compromise that will allow your king the chance to be happy."

She snorted, a smirk lifting her rather thin lips. "You'd be surprised how many MPs do *not* have your happiness to heart."

"No," he murmured, "I don't think I would. But you, I trust, are not one of their number."

She scowled at him. "I am when you make my job more difficult."

"I promise to behave with the utmost affability."

"You'll do no such thing." She drummed her fingers on her desk. "In a way, I *am* pleased by this turn-up. Affording the Reys more power isn't something that I believe is in the best interests of the country. Ferran Rey has his eye on my job."

Bas chuckled. "Then he should be pleased his daughter is no longer in line to be Queen Consort. He'd never be allowed the chance under that kind of conflict of interest."

She blinked at him. "Damn it. I've been so focused on the mess that your cousin stirred up with his South Abarran husband that it never occurred to me. *That's* why the conservatives have been pushing through those incremental changes in the governmental infrastructure. They're leading up to striking the nepotism amendment, precisely so that Ferran Rey *could* be Prime Minister."

"Ah, the nepotism amendment. Another thing for which we must thank dear Louis IV."

"Nothing promotes progress like a tyrant. The boomerang effect is a godsend to my party."

"Then you should have been first in line to annul that infernal contract when I petitioned for it after I took the throne."

"Sorry, Your Majesty. Your late father liked to flex his muscles, if you don't mind my saying, but he never ascended to true authoritarian demagogue status."

"Except where I was concerned," Bas said dryly.

She smiled, a twinkle in her gray eyes. "To be honest, everyone assumed you deserved it."

"Lovely."

The intercom on Isabel's desk buzzed. "Pardon me, Prime Minister."

Isabel glanced at Bas, then punched the speaker button. "Yes, Amabel?"

"There are a few...gentlemen here to see you and His Majesty."

Bas's inclination was to fidget at the potential threat—could the "gentlemen" be opposition leaders? The Minister of Powers?—but he never fidgeted. At least the "gentlemen" moniker meant the visitors didn't include his mother.

"His Majesty and I are occupied. They will have to return later."

"One of them *claims* to be His Majesty's fiancé?"

Bas's eyebrows shot up. Nico? What was he doing here? The notion of Nico having to run the gauntlet of all those Royals—hostile or not—made his blood curdle. "Who are the other gentlemen?"

"Just one other. It's Mr. Vidal."

Bas's stomach lurched. "Just one?" He leaped out of his chair. "What in blazes is he *thinking*? What is Pascal thinking? He can't—" He raced across the room, ignoring

Isabel calling his name, and wrenched the door open. He'd only run six feet, but it felt like miles the way his breath was sawing in his chest.

He lurched through the door, his teeth bared, ready to do battle. "What do you think—" He stopped, faced with four identical expressions of slack-jawed shock on Amabel, Vidal, Nico—and Pascal. "Pascal. You're here."

Pascal, to his credit, recovered the stoic mien that was the hallmark of the palace guards. "Of course, Your Majesty."

Bas tugged on his jacket, even though it didn't need it. "Yes. Well. Good." *What the hell was that about?* He hadn't lost control of his temper since he was a child, not even when faced with the most reactionary of MPs or the most irritating of his relatives, yet the thought of Nico merely walking the halls of the palace—of Bas's *home*—without suitable protection had set him off. *Think about it later.* "I was under the impression that Rozenn—that is, Baroness Savatier had taken you under her wing, my dear."

Vidal recovered his composure next, although his smile was a trifle forced. "She did, Your Majesty. However, I'm afraid something may have slipped your mind."

Bas's gaze flicked from Vidal—was that *smugness* flitting across his face?—to Nico, who was looking rather white around the eyes (as who could blame him), to Amabel's avid expression. His skin still buzzed with unaccustomed agitation, but he tried to draw his usual mantle of calm around him. It didn't seem to fit as well as usual, though, as if his skin had grown too tight for his body. "Have I forgotten an engagement? You must forgive me, Vidal. You know I depend on you to keep me punctual."

"Yes, Your Majesty. I'm afraid you *have* forgotten an *engagement*." Vidal's eyes flicked sideways at Nico, but Bas wasn't able to decipher the cryptic message.

"Perhaps you could enlighten us all, then," Bas said at his most urbane.

"The Sequester, Your Majesty."

Completely unprecedented ice encased Bas's spine. The Sequester was another of Louis's notions—a twenty-four-hour isolation imposed on the monarch and his (or her, presumably, but in North Abarra there had only been kings) betrothed immediately following the public announcement.

Louis had instigated it as a way to test a proposed match to see if the hapless Royal met his expectations before a wedding completely tied his hands. Far too many prospective spouses failed Louis's Sequester and were ushered out of the palace and off to a life of ignominy, some presumably with Louis's bastards in their bellies.

Bas had always hated the stories, including the boasts of his own father. Thanks to the Sequester, Adélard had evaded three different engagements before his marriage to Bas's mother, although Bas's only sibling—that he knew of —wasn't even *that* official.

But as much as the idea rankled, in this case, Bas could embrace it with open arms, because it meant he and Nico would have a chance to get their story straight before their sham relationship was exposed to more intense scrutiny.

Bas donned a more heartfelt smile. "My dear Vidal, I could not possibly forget such a thing." He strode over to Nico and crooked his arm, inviting Nico to take it. "Shall we go?"

The Sequester? What the heck was that? Corin had gotten a manic gleam in his eye and hauled Nico out of his private sitting room—*gah!*—while muttering something in his earpiece, but Nico was too dazed to pay much attention.

Now, as he tucked his hand in Bastien's elbow, he wondered once again what he'd gotten himself into.

A crash. Breaking glass. Angry shouts.

"Nico? Are you all right, my dear?"

Bastien's voice dissipated the vision. Nico blinked and attempted a smile. "Of course."

The Prime Minister scowled from her inner office doorway. "Parliament hasn't confirmed the betrothal, so the Sequester isn't yet in order."

"I beg your pardon, Prime Minister, but Parliament already validated the betrothal when it voted on the contract twenty-six years ago."

"There was no mention of Mr. Pereira in that contract," she groused. Nico had never seen the Prime Minister so… flustered. Well, he hadn't really seen the Prime Minister at all, other than on the broadcasts of Parliamentary procedures or interviews. But while she had always appeared fierce and occasionally annoyed with the opposition, she'd never seemed at a loss before.

"His Majesty's official engagement to his proposed consort was clearly specified, however, and since the announcement was just made publicly, in the presence of a quorum of both North Abarran Royals and Parliament, it's official." Corin held up his tablet. "I checked the protocols. I can forward the case law and parliamentary records to you, if you'd like."

She shot Corin a sour look. "If you would be so kind."

"But in the meantime—" Corin's tablet pinged, and he grinned. "Baroness Savatier says the Sequestrium will be prepared in twenty minutes. In the meantime, if you would please accompany me to the king's private quarters. There are a few details regarding events that I must reschedule over the next twenty-four hours that require your input, Your Majesty."

"Really?" Bastien murmured. "You shock me."

Corin's grin turned a little manic. "Shocks are apparently the order of the day, Your Majesty."

Nico widened his eyes, trying to give Corin the sign to *shut the hell up*, but this was Corin they were talking about.

He never backed down, even when he could clearly see disaster rushing toward them.

So, all right, it was Nico who'd seen the disaster—literally—although in the past those disasters had been minor: the forgotten corkscrew, the misplaced invoice, the delivery delay. They'd never involved broken glass and the sound of an angry mob before.

What's happening to me? It was as if his foresight had expanded beyond things that directly affected him. Well, not *him*, precisely. He never saw himself in his visions. But things he was responsible for. His job. His friends. In their days at the Municipal, the flash of a misplaced textbook had enabled Corin to avoid censure from a vindictive professor and cemented their friendship.

Had this agreement with Bastien expanded the narrow inner circle to include him?

Nico's mind was in a whirl as the five of them—Corin, Gaston, Pascal, Bastien, and Nico himself—made their way through more of those private passages to emerge in the now-familiar hallway. Corin led the way into Bastien's sitting room as Gaston and Pascal took their places outside, on either side of the door.

As soon as Nico and Bastien were inside, Corin shut the door with an ominous click and marched over to the desk. He unlocked a drawer and drew out two sheets of paper. "Here. I suggest you both sign these before the Baroness arrives to run you through the gauntlet."

"The gauntlet?" Nico croaked.

"Every blessed one of the people in the New Palace, from the kitchen staff to Prince Anatole himself, will be lining the halls on the way to the Sequestrium, as tradition demands."

Nico was jolted out of his stupor. "What kind of tradition is *that*? I've never heard of it."

"That's because you're not"—Corin winced—"Royal. Sorry. Plus, there hasn't been a Sequester for forty years, so it's not exactly something that's on everybody's minds."

Nico threw up his hands. "Will somebody *please* tell me what this Sequester is?"

Corin tapped the papers. "Sign first. Explanations can wait."

Bastien sauntered over to the desk, his usual ease obviously returned. Maybe that moment in the Prime Minister's office, when Bastien had resembled Tarik more than Nico could ever have imagined, was simply a momentary aberration. *Or a figment of my overactive imagination.*

But when Bastien picked up the paper, his brows drew together in a frown. "What is this?" He whirled and glared at Nico. "You told him? We agreed that—"

"Calm down, Your Majesty," Corin said, greatly daring from Nico's perspective. "The two of you didn't cover your tracks particularly well. I found your notes."

"You found— Where?" Bastien growled.

"On the desk. Right where you left them," Corin said evenly. "If you don't mind my saying so, Your Majesty, you're rather used to other people carrying the can for you."

Bastien's frown deepened. "'Carrying the can?'"

Nico smiled tightly. "Doing things for you. Taking care of you." He gestured expansively and nearly smacked Bastien in the chest. "Handling things."

"Trailing along behind you to clear away the detritus Royals habitually leave behind."

Bastien's eyes widened at Corin's rather tart tone. "I—" Then he sighed, his shoulders slumping. "That's an entirely fair assessment. We're a sadly entitled lot."

"I should have picked them up," Nico said. "It's my fault."

Corin tossed his tablet on the desk and planted his hands on his hips. "It is *not* your fault. And as far as I'm concerned, it was absolute serendipity." He pointed at Nico's copy of the contract, still on the desk. "You're not going to be able to pull this off without backup. Somebody who can work for you behind the scenes to keep the masquerade going. Someone with deep knowledge of parliamentary law and palace protocols."

"Someone like you, perhaps?" Bastien drawled.

"Well, I *am* the one who invoked the Sequester so the two of you have a chance to breathe." Corin dropped his hands to his sides, suddenly serious. He met Nico's eyes, then shifted his gaze to Bastien. "Do you trust me?"

"Of course!" Nico blurted.

Bastien nodded, dignified as usual. "I always have."

"Then let me help you. I'll do my utmost to keep this between the three of us, but if something happens and we need additional help—"

"Tarik," Bastien said. "If you need more firepower, ask Tarik." Bastien tugged a silver signet off his little finger and passed it to Corin. "Give him this and tell him frog payback. He'll assist you, no questions asked."

"Frog payback? I won't even ask." Corin tucked the signet in the inside pocket of his jacket. "As soon as you both sign these, I'll lock them in the safe. There are no online copies, and I've destroyed the original notes."

"Thank you," Nico murmured.

Corin shrugged. "Even if it weren't my job to...to…"

"Carry the can?" Bastien said blandly.

"Manage your personal affairs," Corin corrected with a mock-scowl, "I'd do it for my friends. And nobody—I mean *nobody*, whether prince or frog—"

"Please don't mention frogs," Bastien said, pinching the bridge of his nose.

"Nobody should be forced into a marriage not of their choosing." He held out a pen to Nico.

Nico took it and picked up the contract. Everything was laid out exactly as he and Bastien had discussed. *Trust Corin to cross all the Ts and dot the Is into the middle of next week.* He signed his name, then exchanged copies with Bastien so their signatures were appended to both contracts.

But even though the pens were no longer moving across the paper, a scratching sound continued. Nico glanced around as Corin affixed the official seal to both contracts and tucked them into envelopes.

"Where is that—" A pitiful mew emanated from…inside the desk?

"Oh my God," Corin breathed. "Polita!" He yanked the desk drawer open to reveal the kitten glaring at them with flattened ears.

"Why did you lock her in the drawer?" Nico asked.

"I didn't! Not on purpose, anyway. She was pouncing on everything and then started rooting around in the drawer, but when I checked, she was asleep and I forgot about her when you showed up."

She scrambled out and scampered over to Bastien, peering up at him as her little bottom wiggled.

"Careful," Nico said, "she's going to—"

Too late. She leaped, but only managed to make it halfway up Bastien's thigh. "Blast! Small but mighty, aren't you, little one?" He disengaged her and held her against his chest, giving Nico a rueful smile. "I suppose I should be grateful her range wasn't a bit longer, or the Sequester would be rather anticlimactic." His eyes widened. "I didn't mean… I mean, I know this isn't a real engagement, and therefore the Sequester isn't a real Sequester, so there's no expectation of… I mean, we say that right in the contract." He frowned. "Don't we?"

Butterflies caromed around Nico's belly. "Will one of you please tell me what a fricking Sequester is?"

Bastien's expression closed. "Another legacy from the Mad King. Essentially, Royally sanctioned premarital sex."

"W-what?" Nico said faintly.

"Our dear Louis wanted to give his prospective consorts a test drive before he committed."

"But wasn't the betrothal a commitment?" Nico asked, bewildered—and if he were honest with himself, a little excited. "Especially in those days, breaking an engagement was—"

"Only a disaster for the prospective consort." Bastien's tone held disgust. "Louis, as was his wont, escaped any censure when he repudiated her at any point prior to the wedding." He smiled tightly. "That was one of the many reasons the country finally had enough of him and deposed the bastard."

"So why wasn't the Sequester eliminated?"

"I have no idea. Maybe it was neglected because there were so many other things in Louis's legacy that were worse. His son, Louis V, was already married, so it didn't even come up until *his* son was betrothed, when an overly diligent Crown's Chamberlain insisted the protocols be preserved. Possibly because nobody liked Louis VI's prospective bride. I think they were hoping he'd repudiate her." Bastien lifted an eyebrow. "He didn't, and a good thing, too. Queen Consort Constanzia was probably the only person on the planet who had a hope of keeping Louis VI in line. He was far too much like his grandfather, except for one thing." Bastien shrugged "He actually loved his wife. And since she put her foot down about their sons' names, Louis VI was the last Louis North Abarra had to suffer through."

Nico was still stuck on the whole *sanctioned premarital sex* thing. "So this Sequester—"

"Is purely so you both can get your stories straight and strategize your moves until you break the engagement." Corin smirked at them. "Although I don't believe the contract prohibits any *private* activities the two of you do or do not engage in."

Nico's face flamed hotter than the fire crackling in the grate. "Corin!"

"Let's just say that what happens during the contract, *stays* during the contract. Now *that* is definitely spelled out. Nothing will follow either of you after its termination, as long as everything that occurs is consensual."

Nico glared at Corin. He should never have mentioned his stupid crush on the king. Trust Corin to try to "help" Nico by setting up a Royal booty call.

Corin folded the contracts and tucked them inside his jacket. "But now, you have a gauntlet to run. Are you ready?"

Nico made himself nod, but kept a tight rein on his thoughts, because he didn't want to ask the question and have his foresight deliver an answer he didn't want.

Or worse, one that he did.

CHAPTER SEVEN

As Bas stood outside the double doors leading to the rotunda, he glanced over at Nico by his side. He'd rather expected the poor man to look terrified by what was about to happen. God knows Bas was terrified, not that he'd ever show it. Although Bas's terror had a different source than what he imagined Nico's to be.

Nico was about to be paraded past every North Abarran Royal, every member of Parliament, the entire New Palace staff, and the entire palace press corps. That was bound to be overwhelming for somebody whose only concerns yesterday were whether he'd brought sufficient cases of wine for the tasting ceremony.

Bas's terror had an entirely different source: Facing twenty-four hours of privacy with a man he found remarkably appealing, could he manage *not* to become his ancestor?

Don't be a fool. You're not a victim of your own desires. You have willpower. But he also had Louis's DNA baked into every cell. He could only hope his ludicrously insignificant power would enable him to maintain his civilized veneer and not send Nico fleeing for the hills.

Nico, however, didn't look terrified in the least. He looked...determined? Stoic? He was staring straight ahead, his jaw tight, as if he were about to face some refined modern torture but was determined to be brave about it.

He patted Nico's hand where it rested on his arm. "Nervous?"

Nico turned his head toward Bas, the lenses of his glasses glinting in the sunlight pouring through the tall windows. "If you'll pardon me for saying so, Your Majesty, that's an incredibly stupid question."

Bas barked a laugh. "Fair point. It won't be so bad."

Nico's eyebrow lifted, skepticism written all over his face. "Really?"

"No. It will be dreadful. But it won't last forever, and then we'll have an entire twenty-four hours when we won't have to see any of them. Which, as far as I'm concerned, is totally worth the next thirty minutes of torture."

"Thirty minutes?" Nico's voice was strangled. "It doesn't take that long to walk the entire length of the palace. Twice."

"True. But we can't move at your usual pace. We must *progress.* Royally."

Nico's eyes narrowed. "You're enjoying this, aren't you, Your Majesty?"

Bas relented, taking both of Nico's his hands in his. "If you mean am I enjoying the pomp and fuss and formality, no. But am I enjoying spending time with you? Yes." Bas dropped a kiss on the back of Nico's hand and was rewarded with a flush on the crest of those amazing cheekbones—which tightened his groin to an unfortunate degree, considering he was about to parade down a double row of his peers. "Although I thought we had agreed. No more *Your Majesties.* You're to call me Bastien." Nico jerked a nod as a fanfare trumpeted on the other side of the doors. Bas tucked Nico's hand back under his elbow. "That's our cue."

The doors swung open with nary a creak—this was the New Palace, after all—and Bas stepped forward with Nico at his side and Gaston, Pascal, and the entire phalanx of his guards at his back, his "gracious monarch" smile in place. The flare of flash photography greeted them—the rotunda, as the most public and therefore least prestigious spot, was full of the press and lowest-ranked staff. One reporter was foolish enough to shout a question and was hustled out by one of the guards—the Sequester Progression was not a place for questions or remarks of any kind.

No, the only response onlookers were allowed was a bow or curtsey, and—once he and Nico reached the door of the Sequestrium, which would be flanked by the highest ranking Royals—applause.

So his and Nico's stately walk from the rotunda through a succession of increasingly ornate audience chambers, down the hall of statues, up the grand staircase and across the portrait gallery to the discreet door under a twelfth century tapestry depicting the first Abarran vineyard (occupied by several unlikely unicorns), was silent except for the rustle of clothing and the sound of Bas's heart beating in his ears.

Lady Helena and her parents, the Duke and Duchess of Llívia, were positioned outside the gallery, and with a jolt, Bas realized that until his announcement this morning, the Duke and Duchess would have expected to be stationed in one of the most important spots: As parents of his prospective consort, they'd have been right outside the Sequestrium door, second only to his mother and Anatole. But now, they weren't able to see the door at all.

Bas glanced their way, since he made a point of meeting everyone's eyes. Ferran and Ona Rey might have been waxwork effigies, so unconvincing were their smiles. Helena—well, she was clearly not happy, blotches of hectic color on her pale cheeks, and for that, Bas was sorry. He hadn't wanted to humiliate her. He just didn't want to marry her.

They passed through the trefoil arch into the gallery. Anatole stood on one side of the Sequestrium door, his mother on the other, and as Bas and Nico cleared the archway, Anatole began the applause that traditionally greeted the betrothed pair. Others picked it up, the sound of clapping passing over them and down the hall behind them like a wave.

God, what must those poor women who'd been commandeered by Louis have thought at this point? Once through that door, they'd have had few illusions of what was in store for them, especially those who had the example of their predecessors as dire warnings. Louis had Sequestered with thirteen women—and repudiated every one of them—before the Uprising.

Did each of them believe they'd be the one to persevere? Or were they resigned to their fate, since at that point, the monarchy was absolute? Bas suspected it might have been a combination of both, depending on the particular woman's own sense of self-worth.

Anatole, his mouth pursed like he'd just drunk a quart of unsweetened lemonade, opened the door. Genevieve was peering at Nico, her brow puckered in confusion. Before she could say anything that would make the occasion even more awkward, Bas turned and faced the crowd—all the highest-ranked North Abarran Royals.

"My fiancé and I thank you for the honor of your presence. We will see you in twenty-four hours."

He escorted Nico through the door into the marble-floored vestibule, trusting Gaston to close it behind them and take up his usual position outside. The vestibule functioned as a sort of airlock—their meals would be left here, and should they require anything, those items would be left here as well. But nobody, not even Gaston, could pass the inner door once Bas and Nico entered.

Bas smiled at Nico, whose shoulders had definitely slumped now that they were no longer on Royal display. "Shall we enter?"

Nico glanced at the door. "I certainly don't want to go back out *there*."

Bas chuckled. "Good point." He keyed in the code on the security panel and opened the inner door. "After you."

Nico gave him a nervous smile and then walked inside. Bas followed, letting the door click shut, effectively locking them in together. Alone. For twenty-four hours.

Nico was gazing around the main chamber, wide-eyed. Bas had to admit it was lovely—plush carpet in green and gold featuring the North Abarran Royal crest; tall windows that overlooked the knot garden and hedge maze; one of the ubiquitous marble-mantled fireplaces, the flames crackling merrily in the grate; the table draped with snowy linen and set for tea; the overstuffed sofas and armchairs in gold and green brocade; the orchids and bromeliads that graced the credenzas and every possible flat horizontal surface. And of course, the graceful arch leading into the bedroom with its king-sized four-poster.

Louis had never been particularly subtle.

"It's... It's..." Nico murmured.

"A tad excessive?"

"I was going to say lovely. But you said this hasn't been used for forty years? It's awfully well kept and, you know" —he pointed to the monitors on the partner desk under the windows—"modern."

Bas smiled wryly. "Do you seriously imagine that Baroness Savatier allows any square inch of the New Palace to be neglected by the household staff? Besides, although there hasn't been a Sequester in forty years, my father used this suite for other things. He brought me up here several times, the last on my tenth birthday, although for the life of me I can't remember why." He frowned. "No, that's not true. I had been looking for my mother and couldn't find her. I believe..." He swallowed, suddenly realizing what must have happened. "I believe she must have been hospitalized at the time, recovering from...from..." *A miscarriage. Every visit must have been following a miscarriage, so I wouldn't see the news, wouldn't hear the staff gossip.*

Nico's hand on his arm brought Bas out of his fugue. "It's all right, Bastien." His voice was soft, comforting. "You don't have to say anything. We're only fake fiancés. I'm not owed any secrets."

Bas forced a smile which was more difficult than he should have found it. "You're owed a great deal, for agreeing to rescue me. But there's no reason for me to burden you with old sorrows or regrets."

Nico smiled, a little shyly. "I wouldn't mind. I'm told I'm a good listener."

"I'm sure you are."

"When your father brought you up here, did you have to make that endless trek through the Palace?"

Bas chuckled. "No. There's a secret passage from the king's bedchamber to"—he nodded at the room beyond the arch—"there."

"Of course there's a secret passage," Nico muttered, then his eyes widened. "Do other people know about it? Could somebody get in from that side?"

"No." Bas smiled as he strolled toward the table. "It's a secret passed from father to son. Not even my resourceful private secretary knows about it."

"But now I do."

Bas paused with his hand on the teapot handle. "I... suppose you do. However..." He shrugged. "What happens during the contract stays during the contract. Tea?"

"Thank you. I can pour, if you'd prefer."

"I think we're able to see to our own tea, don't you? I'm not so entitled that I'm not able to serve myself."

"Yes, but I don't mind." Nico grimaced as he glanced around the room, which was surprisingly bare of amusements. "I don't have anything else to do."

Bas considered that. Nico wasn't a laborer, but he wasn't a Royal either. He had a job. A job he was excellent at, if Tarik's gushing compliments were to be believed. "I suppose twenty-four hours of inactivity isn't something you're keen for."

Nico poured them each a cup of tea, but let Bas doctor his own with milk. "I confess it's not something I've ever pursued. I'm not exactly good with leisure."

Bas took his tea over to one of the sofas that flanked the fireplace. "Really? You don't have any leisure activities at all?"

Nico followed, and when he would have sat on the other sofa, Bas patted the cushion next to him instead. To his delight, Nico accepted the invitation and settled beside him. "I don't have a lot of spare time. Most commoners don't, at least not the ones who have to work for a living."

"Ah." Bas sipped his tea. "I suppose you consider us Royals a soft and useless lot."

Nico's eyes popped wide. "No! At least not you. Or Tarik or Sander or Katalin. Granted, I don't know a lot of other Royals personally, but you all work incredibly hard, trying to make things better." He took a sip from his own cup, his hazel eyes twinkling over the gold rim. "Even if it's only one award-winning wine at a time."

Bastien threw back his head and laughed, then set his teacup on the marble table between the sofas. "I believe far more people appreciate the efforts to create those award-winning wines than arcane legal minutiae or endless trade negotiations."

"They may not realize what those minutiae or negotiations do for them," Nico said seriously, "since so many people prefer a concrete thing they can see or hold—"

"Or drink."

Nico grinned. "Or drink. But their lives are affected by what you do, in ways most of them will never realize, even while they reap the benefits."

Bas gazed into Nico's eyes, so earnest and direct, and something shifted in his chest. *What happens during the contract stays during the contract.* "Nico, may I ask you something?"

"Of course."

"May I kiss you?"

Nico's heart did a backflip. "Wh-what?"

Bastien rested his hands on his knees, his fingers relaxed. "You can say no. Physical...shall we say benefits? Well, physical benefits were never part of our agreement, and I wouldn't want you to think I'd lured you here with the same motives as Louis IV with his string of repudiated consort candidates."

Nico licked his dry lips. "Then why?"

Bastien's smile was wry and perhaps a little self-deprecating. "I rather rashly mentioned the L word during the announcement. It would look odd if we weren't at least marginally affectionate with each other, don't you think?"

Nico's back-flipping heart wiped out with a splat. "So just for...verisimilitude?"

"Well, that." Bastien stood, his smile turning into a grimace, an expression Nico had never seen on his face before.

Maybe he doesn't make that face in public. The king never displayed contempt or distaste when it could be exploited by a political rival. In a way, that warmed Nico's heart. If

Bastien felt comfortable enough with him to show his real opinions, his true feelings, that was good, right? It meant he trusted Nico, just as he trusted Corin and Tarik.

"But"—Bastien's gaze dropped to the carpet, and his voice sounded almost cross—"also because I've wanted to kiss you ever since you appeared in the doorway wearing those blasted glasses."

"My glasses?"

Bastien glared at him from under his bunched eyebrows. "You must know that you look bloody adorable in them."

"No, I..." Nico cleared his throat. "I don't like to wear them. I think they make me look..." *Geeky. Weak. Awkward.* Besides, foresight wasn't much use if you couldn't actually *see.* Not that anybody other than Corin would ever know about his foresight, so he supposed it hardly mattered. *But the king thinks they're adorable.* So he stood up, wiping his damp palms on his trousers.

"Whatever you're thinking, you're obviously mistaken." Bastien retreated a step. "They're quite...alluring. *You're* quite alluring." He turned away. "Blast it. Please forget I said that. Please forget I said anything. We can spend the next twenty-four hours playing cribbage or streaming *Bridgerton* or staring out the bloody windows in different rooms. You don't have to—"

"Your Majesty—"

"Bastien," he murmured. "You promised to call me Bastien."

"Bastien." Nico screwed up his courage and prowled across the carpet as if he were Polita pursuing nonexistent carpet fluff.

The king—*Bastien*—wanted to kiss him. Had *asked* to kiss him. This was like his youthful fantasies come to life. Well, perhaps not *all* his youthful fantasies. Many of them didn't involve clothing, and despite Bastien's confession, Nico didn't harbor any illusions that his attraction to Nico was any more than a passing fancy, brought about by proximity, convenience, and perhaps gratitude. But for right now, if he had permission to kiss the king, he wasn't about to say no.

He stopped a mere hands-breadth away from Bastien's back. *So broad.* His fingers twitched with the urge to run his hands along those shoulders, feel the muscles hidden under that pristine uniform, nuzzle the skin peeping from between the high collar and the neat hairline. But that wasn't what he'd been asked. *Maybe later?*

"Bastien?" he murmured.

"Yes?" Bastien's voice was tight, as if he were clenching his teeth.

"May I kiss you?"

Bastien whirled, his eyes wide, and since Nico was standing so close, nearly knocked him over. He grabbed Nico's shoulders to steady him. "I'm sorry. I wasn't expecting you—"

"To stalk you?"

A smile glimmered in Bastien's eyes. "To be so close."

Nico shrugged one shoulder, enjoying the way the weight of Bastien's hands created a resistance. "Can I help it if you're...alluring?"

"Yet I'm not wearing adorable glasses." Bastien's tone was teasing, playful.

"No. You're wearing yet another of your perfectly tailored uniforms that display your body to its best advantage."

Bastien grinned. "How do you know this is its best advantage? Maybe its best advantage is wearing nothing at all." His grin vanished. "I'm sorry. I didn't mean to suggest that—"

"It's all right. I know you're not trying to take advantage of me." Greatly daring, Nico raised one hand and rested it against Bastien's cheek. "After all, how many people can say they've kissed the king?" When Bastien's eyebrows shot up, Nico realized what he'd said. "Not that I would. Say, that is. We have an agreement, and I'd never—"

"Nico." Bastien caught Nico's hand and kept it pressed against his jaw, which was still smooth even halfway through the afternoon. "I know you didn't sign on for this so you could sell your story to the tabloids. And there wouldn't be much to tell, anyway, not if we're—"

"Marginally affectionate in public?"

"Exactly. So let me know what you want. It might be the first time in this blasted suite that the monarch *hasn't* been the one calling the shots, but that's what I'm giving you in return for what you've given me. Total control over our actions for the next twenty-four hours."

Nico's heart resumed its gymnastics routine. "Total control?"

Bastien nodded slowly. "Total."

"In that case..." Nico lifted his chin—he didn't have to lift it far because Bastien was barely an inch taller—and leaned forward. Slowly. So slowly. Because even if he'd been awarded total control, he wasn't an asshole. He didn't take what wasn't offered.

But Bastien wanted to kiss him. He'd *asked* for a kiss.

So a kiss was totally legal.

Bastien's breath ghosted over Nico's skin, a feather touch, but then it stopped, as though Bastien were holding his breath.

Remember this moment. Remember it forever. The crackle of the fire in the grate. The heat of Bastien's skin against his palm. Bastien's scent—citrus, wool, leather—mingled with the scent of lilies from the arrangement on the table. The way Bastien's brown eyes darkened as Nico drew closer. *All of it. Remember it all.*

Then Nico closed the last millimeters between them and pressed his lips to Bastien's. *Warm. Plush. Soft.*

Then Bastien moaned. Unless that was Nico. Or maybe both of them, because suddenly Bastien's arms were around him, holding him close, and Nico's fingers were laced behind Bastien's neck, pulling him into the kiss, not letting him go.

Bastien adjusted his angle and then…and then…

We fit.

Bastien's tongue flickered along Nico's bottom lip and Nico obeyed the request, opening to allow their tongues to tease and stroke and dance. Bastien tasted of wine and desire, power and promise, and Nico never wanted this to end.

He wasn't oblivious—he knew that hard length he felt against his hip wasn't a fricking banana, for God's sake. But he also didn't want to take advantage of his own remarkable good fortune. So with a burst of willpower he didn't believe was possible, he pulled away, gulping air as though he'd spent the last hour underwater.

Bastien started to reach for him, then let his arms drop to his sides. *Letting me have control, just as he promised.*

"I think," Bastien said, his voice strained, "we will have no difficulty presenting an affectionate mien in public."

"No." Nico tugged on his jacket, which seemed to have shrunk three sizes. *Or maybe it's my skin that's shrunk.* "I don't believe we will. But for now, Your Majesty—" Bastien opened his mouth as if to protest, but Nico held up his hands, palms out. "—*Bastien,* I think we should use this time to do exactly what Corin suggested. Breathe. Consider our strategy. Get to know one another. Because as much as I'd like to spend the next twenty-four hours—"

"Twenty-three hours and thirty-nine minutes."

"—kissing you, we do have a deception to pull off. At the very least, we have to remain believably engaged until sundown on your birthday."

"Yes." The heat faded from Bastien's eyes. "Yes. Of course. You're right." He peered at Nico from under his ridiculously long eyelashes. "Did you mean it about the kissing?"

Nico forced himself to give the king a stern look—realizing exactly how presumptuous that was. "You know I did. You couldn't miss the, er, evidence."

Bastien's gaze flicked downward, where Nico's erection was doing its best to challenge his fly. "I'm a big fan of evidence. In fact—"

"Be that as it may," Nico said, overriding the king's words—also unbelievably presumptuous, but what other chance was he likely to have? "Let's have tea and talk about what the next two weeks will bring." He shifted uneasily. His cock was not deflating, probably because Bastien was gazing at Nico's groin and licking his lips. "Does the Sequester require that we wear formal clothing?"

Bastien lifted a brow. "I believe I mentioned what previous monarchs got up to in here. I suspect clothing of any kind wasn't required." He grinned. "Which would be all right with me."

Nico gave him a stern look. "You also mentioned that your father spent time up here when you were a boy. Surely he didn't lounge about in one of those uniforms the entire time. The medals alone would make his back ache."

"I don't think that's what made his back ache," Bastien muttered. But then he sighed. "Let's see what the staff has stocked for us next door. I rather doubt we'll find the remnants of my father's indiscretions up here, let alone any of Louis's detritus."

"I should hope not. Louis's escapades were centuries ago. Surely there wouldn't be anything left from his time."

"You'd be surprised," Bastien muttered as he led the way through the archway into the bedroom.

Nico trailed behind, *not* staring at Bastien's ass. Okay, yes, he was staring at Bastien's ass, but no court in either Abarra would convict him. All the justices would be too busy. Staring at Bastien's ass.

Bastien strode past the foot of the enormous bed to a vast, elaborately carved armoire in some kind of reddish wood. He flung the doors open, revealing several shelves, a bank of drawers, and at least a dozen dressing gowns in D'Aramitz forest green arrayed on padded hangers. Bastien studied the shelves for a moment, then pulled open one drawer after another.

"It appears we have a selection of lounge pants, T-shirts, sweaters"—he flicked one of the dressing gowns—"robes, and assorted undergarments. Most of them might actually fit us." He flicked a glance from Nico's head to his toes and back. "We're of a similar size."

"Up and down, maybe," Nico muttered, "but not side to side."

Bastien grinned. "But as you mentioned, we don't have to be camera ready. Only comfortable." He stepped back and gestured to the armoire's contents like a game show host. "Take your pick."

CHAPTER EIGHT

Bas couldn't remember the last time he'd spent an entire twenty-four hours lounging about in sweats with no looming responsibilities. He tucked Nico closer under his arm, earning a sleepy grumble, and settled the cashmere throw over both of them.

Nico had fallen asleep against Bas's shoulder halfway through *X-Men: Days of Future Past*. Although Bas knew he'd pay for it with exhaustion later in the day, he hadn't fallen asleep himself. He'd stayed awake all night, cuddled with Nico on the sofa, savoring the warmth and trust and uncomplicated sweetness.

All right, so it wasn't precisely *uncomplicated*. Their whole situation was complicated, based as it was on fraud. Bas pushed that thought away. Their *masquerade* wouldn't have been necessary if his father hadn't pulled that draconian stunt and if Parliament hadn't dug their heels in and refused to rescind it.

He glanced down at Nico again. His lips were slightly parted, his eyelashes dark fans against his cheeks, and a lock of brown hair curled over his forehead. Bas swore he could still taste their single kiss, even though they'd had two meals and a plethora of snacks since then as they'd chatted about everything and nothing. But that kiss...*God*.

Bastien wasn't a virgin by a long shot, although most of his experience had been at university, when his father was still on the throne. Once he'd ascended, he'd eschewed any kind of relationship that smacked of royal prerogative or that might promise a permanence that he neither wanted nor was able to offer, not with the betrothal contract still technically in force.

This fake engagement—this Sequester—gave him the perfect opportunity to act on his attraction without ramifications. He and Nico had signed that contract. After his birthday, once Bastien was free of the threat of a lifetime shackled to Helena Rey, they would sever the engagement and go their separate ways, leaving Bastien free to choose his own consort.

He pressed a kiss to the top of Nico's head with a twinge of guilt since Nico wasn't awake to consent. *It's only his hair. Nothing invasive.* And it wouldn't be. It couldn't be. As tempted as Bas was to pursue the "physical benefits" he'd mentioned, half-jokingly, he'd never overstep. Never press. Never *take*. That was something his father would have done. Something Louis would have done. Something 99% of the monarchs between Louis and his father would have done.

But not me. I won't.

Nico snuggled closer with a little sigh, and Bas tightened his arm around the man's shoulders. His cock tried to weigh in on Bas's decision to exert a little willpower, but he ordered it to stand down. He was the king, damn it. He ought to be able to get his body to obey him. *Maybe I need an act of Parliament. Or a chastity belt.*

He let his head fall back on the sofa cushion, squirming a little to rearrange himself. He hadn't had this kind of reaction to anyone of any gender expression since...well... ever. He'd actually been relieved that he didn't seem to have the same sexual drive and determination to...spread his seed, as it were, as his ancestors. He'd considered it an advantage—it allowed him to focus on his job, his people, his country.

But with Nico's warmth seeping into him, thawing the icy core that he maintained precisely so he wouldn't become as promiscuous as his forbears, he wondered if he simply hadn't met the right person yet.

I can choose my own consort. I could choose him. I could simply never break the engagement.

Bas winced. That wasn't what Nico had agreed to, and not keeping his own part of the bargain—the exit strategy that Nico had been so careful to outline, so insistent on— would be tantamount to the same kind of coercion that Louis had been guilty of. No, he had to let Nico go when the time came.

But that doesn't mean I couldn't court him afterward. Nico's exit strategy included a plan for him to leave the country for an unspecified length of time, should the press hound him as the king's ex. Would he stay away for long? Where would he go? Could Bas find a way to escape his duties long enough to join him at some secluded spot so they could be together without media scrutiny?

He snorted softly. Where were they now, if not in a secluded spot? Unfortunately, everybody in the country knew where they were. Gossip columnists were no doubt salivating, wildly speculating about what the two of them were getting up to during the Sequester.

Despite how much he'd enjoyed their time—which was drawing to a close faster than Bas liked to think—perhaps the Sequester, coming as it did on the heels of the announcement, had been a bad idea. It had given the opposition twenty-four hours to mount their counterattacks. They might emerge from the Sequestrium to get slapped with an interdict order.

No. Isabel wouldn't countenance that. If they hadn't annulled the original decree in the last nine years, they wouldn't change direction in less than a day. They were hoist with their own petard. *I wonder what a petard is.* He'd never been much of a Shakespearean scholar. His tastes had run more to science than literature. Maybe he should look it up. Maybe he should—

"Bastien?" Nico shifted against him and blinked sleepily. "Did I fall asleep?"

Bas smiled, just barely keeping himself from dropping another kiss on the top of his head. "You did. But that's all right."

"What time is it?"

Bas glanced at the camelback clock on the mantel. "Nearly eight. We'll need to emerge soon."

"Soon? But we didn't come in here until nearly three. That's seven more hours."

"That seems soon to me."

Nico battled the over-soft sofa cushions to push himself up on one elbow. "Really?"

Bas nodded. "Really. I've enjoyed our time here more than I can say."

"Because you've been dying to watch *Downton Abbey* and *Bridgerton*." Nico smirked. "Admit it."

"I admit nothing of the sort," Bas said haughtily. "I'm the king. I could declare a national holiday in which everyone must binge all fifteen seasons of *Supernatural* if I wanted."

Nico smiled and brushed Bas's hair off his forehead. "You could. But you wouldn't. You're not that kind of person."

Warmth bloomed in Bas's chest. "Thank you." He gazed into Nico's eyes, his throat unexpectedly tight.

Some—the legions who were inexplicably smitten with Helena's beauty among them—might question Nico's appeal. His mouth was perhaps too wide for conventional beauty, although with those plush lips, the more the merrier, in Bas's opinion. His wavy hair was a tad unruly at times— now, for instance, when half of it was smooshed off-kilter from his time sleeping on Bas's chest. His chin might be considered a trifle too pointed. But all those perfect imperfections were what made Bas's breath catch whenever he looked at him, made his nerves tingle at the way Nico fit against him, even when they were doing nothing but debating the relative merits of Regency versus Edwardian historical TV programs or sniping at the improbabilities in the *X-Men* movies.

And their conversations. God, their conversations. Nico was smart and funny and surprisingly astute, although why Bas should be surprised about it was anybody's guess, considering Tarik's constant ravings about Nico's abilities.

"I don't suppose you'd let me kiss you again?"

Nico wrinkled his nose and even without his glasses— which Bastien had removed and set aside when Nico had fallen asleep—he was still the most adorable man on the planet. But the nose-wrinkle was perhaps a bad sign, a non-verbal *no* to Bas's request.

"I'm sorry," Bas murmured. "I don't want to pressure you into—"

Nico shoved himself higher—or tried to, but his hand slipped down the back of the sofa cushions and he landed with an *ooof* on Bas's chest. "No! I mean, yes, I'd like to kiss you again, but maybe not until I, you know, brush my teeth, because, ugh, morning breath."

Bas made a show of inhaling deeply. "You smell lovely to me."

Nico gave him a *get-real* glare, which shouldn't have thrilled Bas as much as it did. But it meant Nico was comfortable with him. That he wasn't thinking about Bas as the king, but only as a man. "You might be able to sell that to Parliament, *Your Majesty*," he said, his tone laced with indignation, "but I'm not buying it. Now…" He struggled to sit up, hampered by the sofa cushions squishing under his hands and knees.

Instead of assisting him, Bas laced his hands behind his own head and simply grinned, enjoying the show.

When Nico finally struggled to his feet—his lounge pants twisted off-kilter and his long-sleeved T-shirt bunched under his arms—Bas started to chuckle at his indignant expression. But the laugh got caught somewhere south of his throat when Nico's rucked-up T-shirt displayed a strip of taut golden skin along a cut hipbone.

God above, I want to do more than kiss him. But giving in to that temptation would lead him down a path he'd sworn never to walk—the path of Royal privilege and entitlement, the path of Louis and his father and nearly every other North Abarran monarch since the Schism.

So he sat up and gestured toward the bathroom. "Please. Be my guest. In the meantime, I'll check for our breakfast delivery, shall I?"

Nico bit his lip. "You don't have to— I mean, that's more my job, isn't it?"

Bas frowned. "Why would that be?"

"Because I'm…staff."

Bas rose to his feet. "You are not my staff. You are now officially my fiancé, and as such, you're entitled to the same rights and privileges in our personal interactions as I am."

Nico blinked, but then his lips firmed. "That's a nice sentiment, Bastien, but we know it's a load of crap."

"Excuse me?"

"I'm your *fake* fiancé. Contractually obligated. That makes me your staff, don't you think?"

Bas stalked toward Nico, but stopped far enough away not to seem a physical threat—he hoped. "I signed the same contract that you did. It doesn't assign a higher value to one affianced partner than the other."

Nico rolled his eyes. "Well, sure, not explicitly. But you're the king. It's kind of implied."

Gotcha. Bas allowed himself a slow smile. "But as you pointed out, *implied* isn't enforceable when the contract language is specific. That's how we managed to land ourselves in this position, isn't it?" When Nico looked as if he were about to object, Bas held up his forefinger. "And this position is one that I'm extremely grateful and absolutely delighted to be in." He let his smile grow into a grin. "I'd be even more delighted if you'd let me kiss you again."

Nico gulped and scrabbled his glasses off the table. "Hold that thought," he croaked and dashed into the bathroom.

Nico shut the bathroom door behind him and leaned against it, panting as if he'd run a freaking marathon. Another kiss? Was that a trick question?

But he'd done his level best since yesterday to remind himself that this was *not* a real engagement, Bastien was *not* his fiancé or his boyfriend or even his friend, really, despite his friendliness. He was the king. The chief executive of North Abarra. The most powerful single person in the whole country.

And Nico was a commoner with a paltry power that was nevertheless illegal. As soon as Bastien was safe from that ridiculous betrothal contract, Nico would go back to his life as the manager of Royal Crest Vineyards and…

His breath caught and his belly rolled over. Would he still be the vineyard manager? He hadn't actually given Tarik much notice that he was checking out to be the king's betrothed, and since nobody other than Corin knew the whole thing was fake, Tarik would believe that Nico had betrayed him. Or at least left him in a very awkward position by not keeping him in the loop. As manager, Nico was responsible for vineyard staffing, and now he was the one who was bailing on his obligations.

"Crap," he muttered. He really should have considered the consequences of his rash decision—all of them. He could end up with no job, and he wasn't likely to have a vast number of other prospects with the stigma of being the king's ex hanging over his head.

But how could he have refused? He couldn't let Bastien be victimized by something he'd never agreed to. That stupid betrothal—between children, for God's sake!—wasn't politically necessary. Bastien devoted so much of himself to North Abarra. He deserved to be happy in his personal life, as unlikely as it was that his personal life would ever be private.

He sighed and pushed himself away from the door, wandering across the unreasonably large bathroom with its huge free-standing tub—which gave Nico far too many *ideas* about how it would feel to loll in a steamy bath between Bastien's legs. *Stop it.*

The marble tile was warm under his bare feet. Radiant floor heating? Somehow he doubted that the Sequestrium had sported something this relatively modern forty years ago. He had a feeling—not that he'd ever mention it to Bastien—that King Adélard had used this suite for something other than the occasional cozy chat with his son.

The marble vanity sported twin sinks. When they'd arrived, toiletries had been arranged neatly atop monogrammed towels beside each one, including sealed toothbrushes, full-sized bars of milled soap with the D'Aramitz crest, and a whole raft of personal care products—because God forbid either of them should re-use a comb or a pair of toenail clippers.

Nico tried—and failed—to ignore the precisely arranged lube (one on each towel, because of course they couldn't share *that* either) and the three—three!—boxes of condoms.

Good grief. What did they imagine the king's powers were? Endless sexual stamina?

Nico paused, his toothbrush half unwrapped. What *were* the king's powers? He'd never heard, not even in that hotbed of gossip, the Municipal dorm. Bastien certainly didn't flaunt them or use them to threaten his political adversaries the way King Adélard had done. Would it be impertinent to ask? If he didn't know, he might inadvertently do something to negate or compromise the king's powers—similar to the way Sander neutralized Tarik's power when they were in close—*cough*—personal contact. What if Nico did something that put Bastien in danger?

Don't be ridiculous. It's not like his foresight could—

"Ack!" Nico stared at his reflection in horror. His hair was sticking up on one side and flattened on the other, he had a pink-edged crease across one cheek, his shirt was practically in his armpits, and his sweatpants were sideways. He fumbled his glasses off his face, if only so that his reflection wouldn't be quite so clear. Maybe he'd look better in soft focus.

He peeked at his reflection. *Nope.*

Sighing, he finished unwrapping his toothbrush and opened the brand new—full-sized—tube of toothpaste, also with the D'Aramitz crest. It hardly mattered how dreadful he looked. It wasn't as though Bastien had chosen him because of his overwhelming personal attraction.

He snorted. "Ath if," he mumbled around the toothbrush.

The way Bastien had looked at him over their meals, when they'd chatted about books and movies and music, as they'd argued about the latest protest. The way Bastien had tucked Nico close to his side, sharing the blanket with him as they'd watched hours of television. *The way he cuddled me when I slept.*

Nico spat and rinsed his mouth. It would be far too easy to fall into this fantasy, to believe that this engagement meant more than it did, to dream of what would happen if Bastien really *did* fall in love with him and decide to make their engagement real.

Nico glared at himself in the mirror. "Like that would *ever* happen." He tried to mash his hair flat. No luck. He glanced at the corner opposite the tub where a glass-walled shower big enough to hold a half dozen of the king's massive guards beckoned to him.

Oh, why not? They still had a few hours left to go, and it wasn't as though they were about to go crazy, break open the lube and decimate the condom stockpile.

So he stripped and climbed under the rainfall shower head, letting the hot water sluice over his chest and his back, tilting his head and lifting his face to the gentle stream. It was orders of magnitude different from the tiny stall in his apartment near the vineyards. He might as well enjoy the perks of being a fake fiancé while he could.

But as he dried off with the criminally plush monogrammed towels in D'Aramitz forest green, he realized his tactical error: He'd forgotten to bring a change of clothing. Well, not forgotten. He hadn't planned on a shower until he'd gotten a look at his morning-after appearance.

Good lord. Would they have to parade past the same mass of people on the way out of the Sequestrium as on the way in? Talk about a walk of shame, even if nothing shameful had actually happened.

He cracked the door open. "Bastien?"

"Yes, my dear?" Bastien's voice was warm, but clearly he wasn't standing right outside the door. At the table by the windows, maybe? He'd said he was going to bring in their breakfast.

"Could you, um, maybe bring me a change of clothing?"

Bastien's chuckle grew closer and then he was there, peering through the door crack with a far too appreciative grin on his face. "I don't know." His gaze flicked down Nico's bare chest to the towel wrapped around his waist. "What you're wearing now seems quite lovely."

The relatively cooler air from outside the bathroom was making Nico's nipples peak. Bastien's gaze zeroed in on them and he licked his lips. Under the towel, Nico's cock started to stand up and cheer.

Would it be so bad to indulge in a little more than kisses? They both knew this whole *relationship*, such as it was, had an expiration date. Bastien was caring, gentle, and so freaking hot. Why not let things progress, as long as both of them consented, and went into it with the same expectations?

So Nico opened the door further—it didn't creak ominously, not even a little, which he took as encouragement. Swallowing his nerves, he lifted his hands to the towel, Bastien's gaze heating as he followed the motion.

"Nico?" he whispered. "Are you sure?"

Nico nodded. He tucked his fingers under the edge of the towel and—

Crash!

Nico startled, his hands coming up to shield his face for some stupid reason. Bastien was suddenly there, wrapped around Nico. "Get down!" Bastien followed up the order by pulling Nico to the floor.

Nico peered out over Bastien's shoulder. The tall arched window next to the dining table was shattered, a lone shard breaking free to *clish* onto the glass already littering the carpet. On the table, the teapot was smashed under a large, dark object, the cups scattered and broken. Through the open window, angry chants rose.

"Down with King Bastard!"

"Burn the tyrant!"

"Death to tyranny!"

Through the roaring in his ears, Nico became aware of Bastien cursing, long, low, and fluently. But he couldn't hear clearly.

Because this was his vision. The one that hit him the instant he took Bastien's arm before their stately walk to the Sequestrium yesterday.

No. It can't be. This isn't the kind of visions I have.

His chest was tight, hot, as sobs threatened to break free. *I don't want this. Why is this happening?*

He struggled to escape Bastien's arms, desperate to get away, to be alone. "Let me go."

"Nico. Sweetheart. Please. What if it's a bomb? What if— Blast! Where was Palace security? How could they let this happen?"

"Please, Bastien." Nico's breath sawed, but he couldn't get enough air. "I have to— I need to get up. I need to go."

Bastien's hold loosened, and he peered into Nico's face, his own brow puckered with concern. "Are you all right? Were you hit? I don't think—"

"I'll be fine. Just need to... Can't breathe."

Bastin immediately released him, hurrying to the sofa to retrieve the blanket they'd shared and draping it tenderly around Nico's shoulders. "Stay here. I'll get your clothes."

As Bastien disappeared into the bedroom and Nico huddled on the floor, somebody started pounding on the Sequestrium door.

"Your Majesty!" Nico recognized Gaston's voice. "Your Majesty! You need to open the door."

Bastien strode out of the bedroom, a bundle of clothing in his arms. "One moment, Gaston." He handed the clothes to Nico. "I'd best let him in before he deploys the trebuchet."

Nico managed a shaky smile. "You have a trebuchet?"

"Not officially." He smiled tightly. "But Gaston has resources." He stroked Nico's damp hair back from his forehead. "Are you all right?"

Nico nodded. "Just need a little quiet time."

Bastien's gaze flicked from the broken window to the Sequestrium door. "Just as well. I suspect I'll be busy with the security team for the next little while." He stared into Nico's eyes. "Pascal will escort you to your quarters. I want you to stay there, understand? The only people you should let in are me or Corin." Nico nodded numbly. It wasn't as if he was dying to party with dozens of people at the moment. "I'll come to you as soon as I can."

Nico nodded. "I'd like that."

Iron, tangled like writhing snakes. A plinth, tilted. The heavy dark mass falling, falling, falling.

Nico grabbed Bastien's arm. "Don't walk through the hall of statues."

Bastien peered at him quizzically, although he winced when Gaston resumed pounding on the door. "It's hard to avoid. Why?"

But Nico couldn't confess, couldn't tell him why, because he'd expose not only himself, but potentially other commoners with illegal powers. "Just...don't."

"Very well. I won't." Bastien kissed Nico's forehead. "For you."

CHAPTER NINE

Bas closed the bathroom door softly to allow Nico to dress in private. From the sound of things, Gaston was clearly in the vestibule, also clearly breathing fire. Bas almost laughed. Thank goodness no supo had manifested *that* particular power. He punched the code into the control panel.

"Your Majesty. If you don't let me in right this instant—"

Bas flung the door open. "You'll what?" He expected Gaston to charge into the room and begin issuing orders immediately, but instead he stopped in front of Bas, raking him with a nearly panicked gaze.

"Are you all right?"

"My goodness, Gaston, I'd almost believe you cared."

He scowled. "Don't joke. *Are* you all right?"

"Yes, of course. Not a scratch." He nodded toward the bathroom. "We were across the room when it…" His voice faded when he faced the broken window, his belly cramping. *The glass. The table. The enormous rock that had come crashing through.* Nico sat *right there* when they ate their meals. If he hadn't taken a shower, if he hadn't forgotten his clothing, he'd have been directly in the path of the projectile.

Bas swayed on his feet.

"Your Majesty!" Gaston gripped his shoulders. "You're not all right."

Bas took a shaky breath. "No. I am. Just a bit dizzy imagining what could have... What almost..." He stepped back, causing Gaston to drop his hands, as anger banished his fear. Nobody—*nobody*—was permitted to threaten Nico. God, if this farce of Bas's making had put Nico in the crosshairs, he'd never forgive himself.

He met Gaston's gaze. "Has the Palace been cleared of nonessential personnel?"

"All tours have been canceled. Reporters have been relocated to a temporary press room outside palace grounds. All guests have been requested to return to their quarters."

Bas lifted an eyebrow. "Did they comply?"

Gaston smirked. "Since their quarters all face the inner courtyard and not the outer wall? Of course they did, lest the rabble target them as well. Don't worry. You've got a clear shot from here to your quarters."

I'd have had a clear shot in any case. But Gaston didn't know about the secret passage, and though Bas trusted him implicitly, that wasn't knowledge he was willing to share with anyone outside his immediate family.

You shared it with Nico.

Bas brushed the thought aside. "Good." Nico peeked out of the bathroom and Bas smiled in what he hoped was a reassuring manner, beckoning him over. "Nico, my dear, Pascal will escort you back to your quarters."

Nico glanced from the wreckage on the table to Gaston looming at the door, a worry wrinkle pleating his forehead. "Will there be a lot of people—"

"No." Bas had a sudden urge to soothe that wrinkle with kisses, but instead he took Nico's hand. "Gaston and his team have cleared the way. And remember, once you're there—"

"I know. Admit no one except you and Corin."

"Exactly." Bas gave in to his urge and kissed Nico softly. "Until we get the all-clear."

Nico nodded, and Gaston stood aside to let him pass and join Pascal in the vestibule.

Bas sighed as he watched them cross the galley and pass beneath the vast portrait of his father. He'd hoped for another few hours with his fiancé before—

Not my fiancé. Why couldn't he keep that in his blasted mind?

He was hit by a flash of memory. When he was a pre-teen, his mother was having difficulty with one of her household. The Queen's entourage was populated by Parliament, not necessarily by the Queen's own preference, and one of her attendants wasn't who she'd have chosen. Bas had been in his surly, rebellious phase at the time—not that anybody could tell, since he hid it as well then as he did now—and had demanded why she didn't insist that the woman be replaced.

Genevieve had sighed and then smiled at him affectionately. "Can you guarantee the replacement would not be worse?"

"Well." Considering the opposition was firmly entrenched in Parliament at the time. "No."

"Precisely."

"But how can you stand it, Mother?"

"I simply pretend that she's equal to the job. Half the challenge of succeeding at anything is having others believe that you're able."

As it turned out, that same attendant stayed with his mother for years, and became more loyal to her than the attendants his father had picked for her himself.

Would this charade—*pretending* that Nico was his future consort—turn into something similar? Would acting as though Nico was his love match turn it into reality?

He shook the thought off. He had more critical things to consider now. *Nico's safety, for one.* He started for the door, but Gaston cleared his throat. "Did you have something to say, Gaston?"

Gaston grimaced, rubbing the back of his neck. "Are you sure you don't want to...change, Your Majesty?"

Bas glanced down at his outfit. Sweatpants and a royal blue crew-necked sweater, even though it was cashmere, were hardly his customary wear. But sod it, somebody had attacked him. Attacked Nico. "No. Let's go."

He strode out the door and through the gallery, repressing the urge to flip off his father's portrait. "Ask His Grace of Arles to meet me in my office." Bas needed Tarik to scan the airwaves and search for clues about the attack, who might be claiming credit, the reason behind it.

"Already done, Your Majesty. He's—"

"Right here." Tarik appeared in the archway.

Bas didn't even lift an eyebrow. "What took you so long?" He expected Tarik to respond with a *Fuck you* or some similar colorful, Tarik-like rejoinder, but he just fell into step next to Bas.

"The airwaves are going crazy," he said, matching the length of Bas's strides as they powered toward the grand staircase. "Accusations flying, but they seem to be coming from all sides."

"What do you mean?"

"I mean nobody's taking credit and everybody's blaming everyone else. It's as though whoever mounted the protest had no agenda whatsoever."

"Other than heaving a boulder through the Sequestrium window," Bas growled as they plunged down the stairs.

"Well, yeah. That. But after chanting for another few minutes, the crowd dissipated." Tarik turned left into the hall of statues. "I've got..." He stared at Bas, who was standing at the corridor intersection. "What's the matter?"

"I…" *I promised Nico I wouldn't go through here.* "Let's go through the ballroom instead."

Tarik frowned at him, obviously perplexed. "That's not exactly the direct route. Don't you want to get things moving?"

"Yes, but…" How to explain something that Bas didn't understand himself?

Gaston cleared his throat again. "Pardon me, Your Majesty, but the other routes are blocked at the moment while my team secures the area."

Bas glanced down the empty corridor. Ordinarily, the hall of statues was one of the busiest spots in the Palace, since it was not only a central thoroughfare but also the site of some of the most famous sculptures in North Abarra. Today, though, the only inhabitants were marble, metal, and glass.

I know I promised. But Nico will never know. Besides, he had Tarik and Gaston with him. What could happen?

"Very well." He strode down the hall, nearly running, although he realized exactly how ridiculous that was. *Just because I try to get through the place quickly doesn't negate the fact that I was here.* They reached the middle of the hall where the corridor branched off toward his public offices on one side and the solarium on the other. *The solarium.* His mother's favorite room. Did she even know about the attack? "Gaston, if you would be so kind, would you please check on my mother?"

Gaston hesitated. "I should stay with you, Your Majesty."

Bas waved him on. "I've got Tarik with me and my office is two steps away. I assume you've already secured it?"

Gaston drew himself up to his full impressive height, clearly offended. "Of course."

"Then you have nothing to worry about. Please. I'd rather you had eyes on my mother. Take her to my private sitting room, please. I'll be able to concentrate better if I know she's safe."

Gaston nodded and strode off toward the solarium.

Bas gazed at his retreating back, wondering whether he dared introduce his mother to Nico.

"Bas? Are you coming or not?"

Bas turned back at Tarik's impatient tone. "Of course. Now if you—

A hideous screech cut off Bas's words, and Tarik's eyes widened in horror. "Look out!"

Tarik lunged toward Bas, but before he'd gotten two paces, the larger-than-life statue of Medusa *whoosh*ed past Bas's nose to crash to the floor inches from his feet.

Bas's breath was frozen in his chest as he stared at the fallen sculpture. It was mostly intact—the thing was made primarily of cast iron, for pity's sake—but pieces of its unfortunate hairdo had broken off in the fall. For some reason, the only thing Bas could think of was *how can I keep this from Nico?* Black spots danced in his vision as he gulped in air. "You know," he croaked, "I never liked that statue. I hadn't realized it returned the sentiment."

"Holy fucking shit," Tarik murmured as he bent over and retrieved a newly severed snake head, its protruding tongue bent at an odd angle. "This thing must way a fucking ton."

Snakes. Why was it always snakes? "Really, Tarik. Your language."

Tarik, as usual, paid no attention to Bas's rebuke. Instead, he hefted the broken piece in his hand for a moment—and then launched it straight at Bas's face.

Bas didn't even have a chance to register the attack, let alone dodge, shocked as he was that it was Tarik doing the attacking. *I'll have a black eye at my birthday ball.* But instead of hitting him, the snake head inexplicably missed him completely, a whoosh of air ruffling his hair as it passed to smash against the wall.

"What the bloody—" Bas's stomach plummeted and he lunged for Tarik, grappling with him, his hand at his cousin's throat. "Mastermind," he growled, "get out of his head or I'll—"

"Chill, Bas." Tarik was grinning like a fool, undeniable proof that Mastermind must have overtaken him again, as he'd done at Tarik's wedding. "It's me."

"That's exactly what Mastermind would say." Bas's teeth ached from clenching them. "I'll throw you in the dungeons —"

Tarik didn't stop grinning. "The real dungeons, or the ones you and I built under the state dining table with Anatole's shoeboxes when you were six and I was eight?"

Bas blinked. Nobody knew about that. Nobody except him, Tarik, and Rozenn, who'd threatened them with the worst fate she could imagine—a permanent embargo of the chef's nutmeg scones. He loosened his grip. "Tarik?"

"That's right. Mastermind can stuff shit into someone's mind, but he can't extract anything."

"Then why in blazes did you just try to brain me with a cast iron snake head?"

Tarik's grin grew even wider. "Paired powers." He buffeted Bas's shoulder. "Your fiancé supercharged you, Bas. That statue was heading straight for you. I couldn't have reached you in time. It would have squashed you like a bug."

Bas peered at the statue. "Surely not."

"I *saw* it. It started to fall, and then it took a hard left in the air. I may not be the brightest scientist on the planet, but even I know gravity doesn't work that way." He grinned wider, which Bas hadn't thought possible. "You deflected it, Bas, just like you deflected Medusa's ex-curl just now. Congratulations, cousin. You're invulnerable."

Pascal opened the door to Nico's sitting room. "Thank you, Pascal."

"My pleasure, sir."

Nico trudged inside—and was immediately torpedoed by a ball of what appeared to be animate fluff. He disengaged Polita's claws from his leg—*ow!*—and cradled her against his chest. "I'm not entirely sure why you're here and not with Corin—"

"Because Corin is here too." Corin emerged from the bathroom, drying his hands on one of those ubiquitous green monogrammed towels. "Along with Her Royal Highness Polita's food dishes and—fortunately or unfortunately, depending on your point of view—her litter box."

Polita scrambled up Nico's chest—*more ow!*—and settled on his shoulder, purring away like a fur-covered motorboat. Oddly, her presence comforted him.

"You would not believe the fuss that's been going on," Corin groused as he closed the door to the bathroom. "Snakes! In the official Bonfire Night fire pit. The grounds staff was having a conniption because apparently they're the *venomous* kind and not the type one welcomes into one's garden to control the rodent population."

"Mmmhmmm." Nico rubbed his cheek against Polita's fur.

"Luckily Lady Helena was here and convinced them to leave, although more seem to be slithering in every time she clears out a nest." Corin propped his fists on his hips. "Nico? Are you even *listening* to me?"

Nico stumbled across the room and collapsed onto the sofa, careful not to dislodge Polita. "*Gah!*"

"Nico?" Corin tossed the towel aside and approached him, a worried frown on his face. "What's wrong?"

"My powers," Nico croaked.

"Oh my God." Corin sat next to him. "Did somebody find out? Did the king? Were you threatened?" As usual,

Corin didn't wait for Nico to respond. "Of course nobody found out. It they had, you'd be in jail."

"Nobody's found out. But they've changed."

Corin's jaw dropped. "Changed? How? They've been stable ever since I've known you."

Nico shot him an irritated glance. "You think I don't know that? But, Corin, the attack…" He swiveled to face Corin, pulling one knee onto the sofa. "I saw it."

"You saw it?"

"Stop repeating what I say!"

"Then start making sense! What do you mean you saw the attack? You've only ever seen individual *things* before, like that copy of the book that had the exact reference I needed to make my case for this job."

"I *know*. But this time I didn't just *see*, I *heard*. The crash. The breaking glass. Th—the chants of the crowd." *Down with King Bastard. Burn the tyrant. Death to tyranny.* "The instant I touched Bas's arm before we progressed to the Sequestrium, I saw it all." He swallowed convulsively. "And then, before we left the Sequestrium, I saw something else."

"What?" Corin whispered.

"A sculpture. That big one in the hall of statues. Medusa. I saw it fall."

Corin's brow knotted in confusion. "That's impossible. The thing must weigh a ton. I think they had to reinforce the floor so it wouldn't fall through into the bowling alley."

Nico blinked. "There's a bowling alley?"

"Stick to the point. How did your powers used to work? How did you know I needed that book, or that Tarik needed whatever he forgot to bring with him last, because God knows that man needs a keeper."

"He's got all those voices in his head," Nico said indignantly. "That would distract anybody."

Corin waved one hand. "Never mind that. How do you invoke your powers?"

"I don't really *invoke* them. Not intentionally, anyway." Nico thought about how his foresight manifested. "I just get a flash of something. Like that book. Or a vendor invoice. Or the corkscrew that Tarik needed for the ceremony yesterday." He petted Polita absently. "I don't consciously think, *What would Corin need to nail the interview*, or *What do I need to prove we paid this invoice two months ago*, or *What will Tarik need for the ceremony*. It's more like...the book was needed by you, or the corkscrew was needed by Tarik." He slumped against the sofa cushions. "God damn it. I've got a freaking *passive voice* power."

Corin tapped a finger on his crooked front tooth, something he always did when he was thinking hard. "I'm not so sure. Maybe it's only been passive because *you've* been passive. Do you actively ask it questions?"

"No. Of course not." He pouted. He could own it. "I don't like to *encourage* it. What if I used it at some point when one of those Ministry of Powers undersecretaries was snooping around with their calibration gadgets?"

"Maybe you *should* encourage it. I know I had to practice with mine before I could control them sufficiently to make them super useful." He smirked. "Super useful superpowers. Get it?"

"Shut up. Maybe mine aren't useful at all. I mean, I saw the attack, but I couldn't *do* anything about it."

"Did you try?"

"No. How could I? I didn't even know what it meant!"

"Keep your shirt on." *Tap tap tap.* "Okay, what about the other vision? The one with the sculpture? What were you doing when you saw that?"

Nico blushed, because he'd been mostly naked with Bastien at the time. Corin, of course, caught it because of course he would, so before he could make a comment, Nico rushed on to say, "Bastien had said he'd come to meet me. Then I saw the statue falling."

"But you didn't see it landing?"

"No. Just falling. I...um...warned the king not to walk through the hall of statues."

"Do you think he obeyed?"

Nico's face heated further as he remembered Bastien's soft *For you* and the accompanying kiss. "He said he would."

"Well then..." Corin's gaze turned distant, the way it always did when he was listening to his headset. His jaw dropped. "Holy shit," he murmured, turning his suddenly intense gaze on Nico. "Medusa just took a header off her plinth."

Horror seized Nico by the throat. He grabbed Corin's arm, earning a protesting mew from Polita. "Bastien. Is he —"

"He's fine. It missed him."

Nico was unprepared for the wave of anger that swept through him. "I *told* him not to go that way. He *promised*."

Corin blinked at him. "Ooookay."

"I *hate* this power." Nico leaped to his feet and paced across the room, Polita hissing in protest as she dug her claws into his jacket. "What good is it? I see these things—things I don't ask for—and then can't do anything about them? This *sucks*! I have to experience the same trauma twice!"

Corin stood and approached him as if Nico were a bomb about to ignite—which wasn't that far off. "How do you know you can't do anything about it? Have you tried?"

"Yes! Didn't I just say that I told Bastien not to walk through the hall of statues?"

"Setting aside the fact that you're calling the king by his first name for a moment—"

"He asked me to. For...for verisimilitude."

"Uh huh. Well, setting that aside, did you tell him why?"

Nico scowled. "Of course not! I couldn't expose my powers to him." He jabbed Corin in the chest. "And not just because it would land me in jail. It could affect you and every other powered commoner in both countries. Our only protection is that nobody knows about us."

"Or maybe they're just in denial," Corin drawled. Then he straightened his shoulders. "You need to practice."

"Practice?"

"Find out how it works. Find out if you *can* make a choice."

Nico choked back a hot rejoinder. *A choice?* Could it be so simple? If he hadn't taken Bastien's arm, and walked the gauntlet as his fiancé, would the attack have occurred? If Bastien hadn't promised to join Nico, would the statue have fallen?

"Crap," he muttered. "This is turning into one of those pointless metaphysical brain pretzels. If a tree falls in the forest and there's nobody to hear it, does it make a noise?"

Corin lifted an eyebrow. "Maybe you should be more concerned over ensuring nobody's in the forest so they don't get smooshed by the tree."

Nico scowled. "It's a hypothetical tree. And a hypothetical forest."

"Well, they're hypothetical people too, so where's the problem?"

"The problem," Nico ground out between clenched teeth, "is that the people might not be hypothetical at all. Bastien isn't hypothetical and that statue that nearly flattened him wasn't hypoth—"

The breath left Nico's lungs, and he crumpled onto the sofa again. Bastien had almost been killed, or at least badly injured. If he had been clearer, if he had told Bastien the truth, maybe he would have stayed away from the hall, stayed safe. If Nico hadn't been so worried about protecting his own hide, if he'd told Bastien who he was, how he really felt—

"Nico. Nico!"

Nico blinked, the room coming back into focus. Corin was kneeling on the carpet in front of him, worry creasing his brow, and Polita was kneading his thigh, her purr amped up to eleven. "What?"

"He's okay. The king wasn't injured. It's not your fault."

"Isn't it?" Nico sucked in a breath, but it didn't seem to help his dizziness. He dropped his gaze, unable to meet Corin's eyes, and focused on the bright orange fur on Polita's left ear.

Is it like a crossroads? Could he pick the road he wanted, seek the outcome he craved? Or was everything fixed? He rubbed his eyes. Life couldn't be that binary, could it? It wasn't as simple as *do I walk down this corridor or that one,* or *should I say yes to the king or no?* And okay, maybe life wasn't binary, but his power probably was. And it didn't exactly present him with a lot of options.

Or maybe it had, and he'd never paid attention. Maybe his powers weren't changing at all. Maybe he'd never had anything that *mattered* to him as much as Bastien's safety and happiness.

"Nico—"

"Just a minute. I need..." He swallowed. "I need a minute. Please."

To his credit, Corin backed off, leaving Nico huddled on the sofa with Polita in his lap. He bowed his head and closed his eyes. How to phrase the question, that was the problem. It couldn't be anything too big, like *what happens if I— Whoops.* Now he was afraid to even ask the question in his head, for fear of what he'd see.

Concentrate on something small, something specific. And since Bastien was pretty much consuming all his brain cycles at the moment, he should probably make it Bastien-related.

Okay. I can do this. Bastien had promised to come to him—and suddenly Nico could see him in his mind's eye. Tall, gorgeous, worry darkening his eyes as he gazed at Nico.

"You could have been hurt. I couldn't live with that. Say the word and we end this now."

A choice. Bastien was going to give him a choice. To stay or to go. And then Nico could almost see it, like a fork in the path—or no. Like two doors floating in an amorphous *nothing,* one marked *Stay* and one marked *Go.*

He opened the mental *Go* door, and behind it was his desk at the Royal Crest offices, exactly as he'd left it three days ago. Somehow, his name on the nameplate, with *Manager* embossed in gold below it, didn't give him the usual sense of satisfaction.

In his mind, he pushed the door almost closed and stepped to the other one. Hand shaking, he pulled it open.

Nico's bedroom. Nico's bed. Bastien above him, chest bare, gazing down with eyes heavy lidded and dark with passion.

Nico blinked, the vision fading.

That. I choose that.

As if there were the slightest question. He had committed to this path—*dreamed* of this path—the moment he agreed to be Bastien's fake fiancé.

CHAPTER TEN

Bas rolled his shoulders, trying to ease the tension and the fatigue from hours of frustrating, fruitless investigation. "Still nothing?"

Tarik, slumped on the love seat in Bas's office, cracked an eye open. "Nothing more than the general outrage about you being engaged to a commoner. Nobody's happy about that, apparently. The Royals are outraged that you're flouting our oh-so-sacred traditions and disrespecting Lady Helena. The commoners think you're exploiting them the way—"

"The way Louis did."

Tarik closed his eyes again. "Louis was more egalitarian in his exploitation. The Royals were just as likely to catch his roving and slightly crazed eye, particularly when it came to consort choice. Nothing specific about the attack, though. I'd have told you if there were."

Tarik's brows were bunched, the creases deep between his nose and mouth. Monitoring the airwaves, with all their competing frequencies and incessant traffic, always gave him a massive headache. Since they'd been at this for hours, Tarik was probably barely able to concentrate for the pain. He needed to go off and float in one of the enormous bathtubs in his quarters.

No. He needs his husband. Once in Sander's arms, Tarik could get relief from the cacophony. And possibly another type of relief as well.

Ugh. Although he didn't begrudge his cousin the happiness and sexual fulfillment he'd found with Sander, Bas couldn't help but be envious.

Because he was about to condemn himself to a lifetime of tepid contentment at best. He'd made that decision almost as soon as he'd realized that rock could have killed Nico. The notion that the opposition factions—whoever they were—were resorting to violence to protest this engagement was absolutely intolerable.

If Bas's attempts to get out of an inconvenient and relatively distasteful marriage meant that Nico might be harmed, Bas needed to put an end to this now. Nico's welfare, the welfare of his people and country, were ultimately more important than his own happiness.

Helena couldn't be any more thrilled with the match than he was, although she seemed willing to accept the inevitable. *Hardly a ringing endorsement for a happy marriage.* But he was the king. He had obligations. And she'd expected this match from childhood.

Bas planted his palms on his desk and pushed himself to his feet. "Go back to your quarters, Tarik. Take Sander to bed."

"I can't," he grumbled. "He's at the airport to meet Katalin."

"Why? There's a contingent of guards there to meet her plane."

"Settle down. It's not that he doesn't trust your guards, but Katalin is his sister, and he's gone full Neanderthal protective big brother." A grin banished the wrinkle between Tarik's brows. "I'm so proud."

Bas glanced at the windows. Darkness had fallen, the soft spring night disrupted by the palace security lights. They both needed rest. "Go anyway. There's nothing more we can do here for the moment. Take a bath. Take some painkillers. Take a nap. We'll reconvene tomorrow morning."

Tarik peered at him. Then his eyes widened and he sat straight up. "Don't."

Bas smoothed the uniform jacket he'd donned before his first post-attack meeting with Lady Isabel. "Don't what?"

"You're about to do something really stupid. I can tell."

"I don't know what you're talking about," Bas said in his most urbane tone, although it had a rougher edge than it ever had before.

Tarik surged to his feet. "I've known you since you were in your cradle, Bas. Your bullshit doesn't fly with me. You've got that *look*."

"I'm sure I don't know—"

"Shut the fuck up. You're about to martyr yourself for some asinine notion of the common good. Do *not* break your engagement. It's the best thing that's happened to you since your fucking father died and stopped trying to convince you that you weren't worthy to be king."

Bas stared at Tarik coldly. "If I'm not willing to sacrifice my own convenience for the good of my country, then clearly I'm *not* worthy."

Tarik rolled his eyes and then winced as if the movement hurt. "Give me a fucking break. A contented king, one who isn't tied up in sexual frustration knots, is a damn sight better for the country than one who's perpetually pissed off from blue balls. Even Louis didn't turn into a gigantic dickwad until his first Queen died."

"As charming as your descriptions are, this isn't your decision."

"Maybe not." Tarik jabbed a finger at him. "But let me remind you that it wasn't Helena who activated the powers that just prevented you from being nothing but a stain on the royal carpet. That was Nico." Tarik's eyes narrowed.

"Who's to say those powers won't diminish again if you send him away? Louis nearly tore the country apart in his search for another power to pair with his. Don't fuck this up, Bas. Don't turn into Louis."

Heat built behind Bas's eyes. "That you'd even suggest —"

"Oh, get over yourself." Tarik heaved a heavy sigh. "Louis was probably a few crackers short of a cheese board even before Queen Maria died, but there's no denying her death affected him. You have a chance to be happy, Bas. Happy and powered enough to satisfy every calibration test the Ministry can pull out of its ass. Like I said. Just don't fuck it up." He trudged to the door and walked out, nodding to Gaston as he passed.

Bas sighed. Regardless of Tarik's opinion, it wasn't fair of him to make the decision for Nico. He blinked. Maybe the unilateral decision to terminate the engagement wasn't fair either. Nico should at least have a voice in the matter. *And I'll do my best not to beg him to stay.*

He strode out of the office, Gaston falling into step behind him. The corridors in the governmental wing were no longer empty, but they weren't excessively crowded either, everyone moving with purpose and intent, motivated as they were by the attack. The poor art installation supervisor had suffered through interrogations by everyone from Rozenn to the Prime Minister and still claimed tearfully that he had no idea how that sculpture could have toppled.

"It was bolted to the plinth," he insisted, although Gaston's team had discovered the bolts had been sheared.

"Any more news on the…incident in the hall of statues?"

"No, Your Majesty," Gaston said.

"Very well." Bas paused outside the door to Nico's private quarters where Pascal stood at parade rest. "Is all well here, Pascal?"

He nodded. "Yes, Your Majesty. Mr. Vidal was with Mr. Pereira for some time earlier, but he's returned to his office now."

"Thank you." At least they could have this conversation in private, without having to make an awkward request for Vidal to leave. Bas knocked on the door. "Nico? May I come in?"

The door flew open and there Nico was—his hair tousled, his clothing rumpled, and his glasses—God, his glasses—slightly askew. Polita was riding on his shoulder. He cut a glance between Gaston and Pascal. "Of course, Your Ma—Bastien." He stood aside so Bas could enter and shut the door with a final-sounding *click*. "I was getting worried."

Bas faced him, his fingers twitching with the need to *touch*, to *soothe*—although he wasn't certain who would be soothed more: Nico or himself. "I apologize. There were a great many things to put in motion."

Nico nodded. "Of course."

Bas took a breath, steeling himself. "Nico. I hope you know that I would never knowingly put you in danger. When we agreed to this engagement, this temporary charade, I didn't think it would do any harm to anything except perhaps the political machinations of certain members of Parliament. But it has taken a more sinister turn. One that I didn't foresee—"

For some reason, Nico flinched at the word. *Just as I thought. He doesn't want this either. He didn't sign on for being a target for terrorists.*

"You could have been hurt. I couldn't live with that. Say the word and we end this now." Nico sucked in an obvious breath, his shoulders rising. Bas smiled, perhaps a touch wanly, if only to reassure him. "Other Royals from time out of mind have managed to live perfectly reasonable lives with state marriages. Surely I can do the same."

A smile dawned on Nico's face, punching dimples in both cheeks that Bas had never noticed before, crinkling the corners of his eyes behind those damned enticing glasses. *Here it comes. He's so relieved to be released from this that he's about to burst into laughter.* Or perhaps dance around the room, despite the kitten on his shoulder.

But Nico did neither of those things. Instead, he placed Polita on the floor—much to her evident displeasure—and advanced on Bas until they were bare centimeters apart. Then he ran both hands up Bas's chest and around the back of his neck to tangle in his hair. "I'm staying," he murmured, then angled his head and kissed Bas, slow, sweet, and oh, so intoxicating.

Bas's head spun, but he wasn't so dizzy that he didn't grasp Nico's hips and pull him close, moaning into his mouth, deepening the kiss until he couldn't separate his own breath from Nico's.

This is what a true partnership should be. Not orderly and polite and pallid, but hot and passionate and a little messy. Because love wasn't neat. *Life* wasn't neat. But with the right person beside you, that didn't matter.

With Nico in his arms, Bas could learn to revel in the chaos.

Reluctantly, he drew himself away. "Are you sure? Because—"

"Bastien." Nico ran a finger along Bas's lower lip. "My bedside table is stocked with enough lube and condom packets for a whole platoon of guards."

"Is it?" Bas licked his lips, tasting Nico, a finer vintage than either Abarra could boast.

"Do you suppose we could go use some of them now?" Nico's smile was definitely flirtatious as he glanced up at Bas from beneath his lashes—*and from behind his glasses.*

Heat tore through Bas's veins, his cock nearly strangled behind his far too well-tailored trousers. "I would like nothing more."

Bas tangled his fingers with Nico's and led him through the dressing room and into the bedroom beyond. The bedside lamp cast a golden glow over the snowy pillowcases and the sheets revealed by the Palace's efficient turndown service. The forest green duvet was folded neatly on the tufted velvet bench at the foot of the bed, as if the staff had anticipated that the bed might be used for something other than sleeping.

Clever staff. I must give them a bonus. Or perhaps a knighthood.

Nico halted next to the bed and turned to face Bas. "You're back in your pristine uniform. I'm rather afraid to get you mussed."

"I wouldn't mind being mussed by you, but do you know what would solve that problem more efficiently?" Bas grinned.

"What?"

"This." Bas unbuttoned his jacket faster than he'd ever done in his life and tossed the damn thing across the room.

Nico's eyes widened. "Won't it get wrinkled?"

Bas stripped off his undershirt and sent it after the jacket. "I doubt it. But even if it does, I don't care." He cupped Nico's face between his hands and kissed his lips. "Not if it means I can be naked with you all the sooner."

"Thank goodness," Nico murmured, and began to shed his own clothes as Bas toed off his shoes, then dropped his trousers to the ground and kicked them aside.

Cursing under his breath, he peeled off his socks. When he stood again, Nico was *there*, in front of him, all naked golden skin, soft springy hair, and glorious erect cock—cut, as was the norm for so many commoners.

"God, you're beautiful," Bas murmured.

Nico laughed a little nervously. "I was about to say the same thing."

Bas reached out and slowly drew Nico to him, his breath catching as their chests brushed, their hips aligning, their cocks nestled side by side.

Heaven.

And Bas intended to hold on to it as long as he possibly could.

Nico was certain the king's hungry gaze was about to set his skin on fire.

Bastien nuzzled beneath Nico's ear. "You feel like heaven," he said, his voice rough.

Heaven. Nico wrapped his arms around Bas and sighed. *That's it exactly.* He let his hands explore Bastien's back—the broad wings of his shoulder blades, the smooth muscles along his spine, the curve of his hip. While part of his brain was having a total meltdown—*we're naked! Together!*—the rest of it, along with certain significant parts of his body, was reveling in being with *Bastien.*

Not because he was gorgeous. Not because he was rich. Not because he was the freaking king, for God's sake. But because he was caring and principled and *good.* The perfect man. The kind of man Nico had always dreamed of but never hoped to find.

The kind of man I'm not worthy of.

But for now, in this enchanted pool of light amid the looming darkness of his future as the king's ex, he could pretend. Pretend that he was worthy. Pretend that there wasn't an expiration date on this relationship.

Pretend that he'd eventually get over it and move on.

But when Bastien drew back and gazed into his eyes, his expression intense and yet oh so tender as he carded his fingers through Nico's hair, Nico suspected that he'd never get over it. Never get over *him*.

Because I love him.

Not the country. Not the king. The *man*.

And because he loved him, Nico knew that he'd go quietly when their agreement ended. If it meant he had to leave North Abarra for weeks, months, even years, separating him from the job he'd loved, his home, his friends, he'd do it. Because it meant that Bastien would be happy, that he wouldn't be forced into a match not of his choosing.

Not by his father. Not by Parliament. *And not by me.*

Bastien's brow wrinkled. "What's wrong? Why do you look so sad? If this isn't what you want, we don't—"

"No!" Nico pressed a quick kiss to Bastien's jaw. "I mean, yes, I want this. I want *you*." He scared up a little attitude to hide the truth—that he was head over ears in love with his future ex. "Although I'm a little cross with you right now."

Amazingly enough, Bastien blushed. Nico hadn't ever seen him blush—in fact, he wasn't sure anybody had. Over their regular drink sessions, Corin had groused that the king wasn't capable of looking anything but mildly startled, and even then, not often. *"It makes it really hard to know if I've screwed something up."*

Bastien lowered his gaze to the vicinity of Nico's chin, but then glanced up with the glimmer of a smile. "Because it took so long for me to get here?"

"No." Greatly daring, Nico nipped Bastien's chin. "Because I told you to avoid the hall of statues and you didn't."

Bastien winced, another expression that had never graced his face as far as Nico knew. "I'm sorry about that. But the alternate routes were blocked, and I…" He tilted his head, confusion pinching his brows. "How did you know I did?"

"Corin was with me when he got the message. He told me."

"I admit that events certainly proved out your caution, but why didn't you want me to—"

"Just a feeling," Nico blurted. "I get them sometimes."

Bastien's eyes narrowed. "Are you sure—"

"Absolutely. Just a feeling." Panic sparked in Nico's belly and his cock started to flag. *Deflect. Deflect.* "But I'm very glad it was a false alarm feeling." He forced a smile, although it turned more heartfelt when Bastien flexed his hips in a delicious slide of skin. "Now, I think we were about to conduct a stress test on the lube and—

Skritch skritch skritch.

Bastien's head snapped to the side, his muscles tensing under Nico's hands. "Stay here." He lifted Nico aside, proving that his muscles were for more than show. "If Gaston and Pascal have been compromised—"

"Mew!"

Nico burst into laughter. "Somehow, I doubt that Gaston and Pascal have any sway over that particular intruder. And if I've learned anything about her by now, it's that she's persistent. We might as well let her in."

Bastien shook his head, but gestured for Nico to proceed. "By all means."

Nico walked to the dressing room door, heat infusing his chest and rushing up his neck to his face. "You're staring at my ass, aren't you?"

Bastien chuckled. "Well, it is the most scenic thing in the room. You can hardly blame me."

Although he was secretly pleased, Nico shot a glare over his shoulder. "No objectifying your future ex."

He'd expected Bastien to grin, but the expression on his face could better be described as *arrested*. Or maybe even *regretful*? Nico had never been adept at reading expressions. But he tried not to dive too far down into the *what-does-he-*

mean? weeds. That's wasn't what this relationship was about.

It's not a relationship. He had to keep reminding himself about that. A *relationship* had certain connotations that their agreement did not. They had a contractual arrangement. A *time-limited* contractual arrangement.

Don't project your own feelings. He's the king, for pity's sake, not some guy you met at a bar or a party or through a dating app. There was never any chance for this to go further.

He sighed and opened the dressing room door. Polita pranced into the bedroom, her tail puffed out like a bottle brush. Her pupils were huge and round in the dim light as she glared up at them.

"Nico," Bastien said, a certain amount of trepidation in his tone, "are you sure she's not part demon?"

Nico lifted both eyebrows. "This is reality, Bastien. Demons don't exist."

"Of course. But while I can withstand her claws in my clothing, I'm not certain how parts of my anatomy will react to them."

Nico winced, his hands twitching with the need to cover his groin. But after another disdainful flick of her tail, Polita minced over to Bastien's discarded uniform jacket. After batting at a couple of the medals, she began to knead the dark green fabric, her purr loud in the quiet room.

"No, Polita!" Nico made a break for her, but Bastien was suddenly there, his hand on Nico's arm.

"Let her be."

"But she'll destroy your uniform. She's pulled threads on my best jacket and trousers. The second best too." Polita circled once and settled down in a fluffy ball, her tail over her nose. "At the very least she'll get cat fur all over it."

"Nico, I'd tell you precisely how many uniforms I have, but you might reach the conclusion that I'm vain about my appearance."

Nico recalled the rows of green jackets he'd seen when he'd peeked into Bastien's dressing room. He couldn't hazard a guess at how many there were, but it was a lot. "I wouldn't dare to say you're *vain*, precisely, but you're always so...so *put together*."

"Mere serendipity, along with an excellent tailor and the Palace cleaners." He gestured to Polita. "She seems content now. And as long as she doesn't interrupt when I'm inside you, I don't care." He peered into Nico's eyes. "I mean... That's all right, isn't it? Can I—"

Nico flung himself into Bastien's arms, his cock surging to life again. "Yes! God, yes. *Please*, yes."

Bastien closed his eyes for a moment before he grinned. "Then, my dear fiancé, may I invite you to bed?"

Nico nodded, but when he tried to step away to mount the ridiculously high four-poster, Bastien tightened his embrace.

"First, though, I want to kiss you again. May I?"

Nico snorted. "You're about to fuck me, Bastien. I think we've covered consent."

Bastien's expression turned serious. "That's where you're wrong. Outside this room, I'm the king. I wield perhaps more power and influence than is healthy for any one man. But in here? With you? In here, my dear, *you* rule. Nothing will happen that you don't want, and if I seem to be asking for permission rather more than seems necessary, I'm only attempting to reinforce that dynamic in my own mind."

If Nico hadn't been in love with Bastien before, *that* would have done the trick. But he wanted Bastien to enjoy this, too. To *want* Nico as much as Nico wanted him, even though that seemed highly unlikely. Could a man so accustomed to power willingly yield it to another? Nico started to grin. Maybe there was a way for Bas to hold on to power at the same time he relinquished it.

Bastien's eyes narrowed. "That is one of the most evil grins I've seen outside my cousin Tarik."

"Bastien," Nico said, surprised that his voice could sound quite so throaty and seductive. "Kiss me."

Something flared in Bastien's eyes, but he angled his head and complied, the kiss soft, sensual, and seductive— but not excessively heated. He pulled back and quirked a smile. "Like that?"

Nico pretended to consider. "Adequate. But I think you can do better. This time"—he flicked his tongue across Bastien's collarbone—"put a little effort into it."

"Effort?" Bastien's tone was laced with mock outrage. "I'll show you *effort*."

He cupped Nico's face in both hands, his grip not precisely gentle, and positively *dove* for Nico's mouth. Lips, tongue, teeth. The scrape of end-of-day beard abrading Nico's skin. *As mine is probably doing to his.* The notion of his own beard burn on Bastien's face sent a surge of heat from the top of Nico's head to his heels—and every point in between. He drew back on a gasp to check—because apparently he was a possessive asshole. *There.* The reddening under Bastien's lip, on his cheek, his chin. Nico touched it with a fingertip.

"I've marked you," he murmured.

Bastien blinked. "You have?"

"Don't sound so surprised." He rubbed his own tingling skin. "You've done the same to me."

"But I've never— No one has ever—"

"Never mind that now." Nico backed out of Bastien's embrace, chuckling at Bastien's whimper of protest. "At the moment..." He climbed onto the bed on his hands and knees. He dropped his forehead to the sheets, his ass in the air. "Prep me. Nice and slow. Plenty of lube. But I want to feel at least three fingers before you fuck me." Nico dared a glance over his shoulder and his belly clenched. Bastien looked stunned, jaw sagging, eyes wide. "If you're very good, I'll keep my glasses on."

Nico shivered at the heat in Bastien's eyes. "Your command, my dear, is precisely my wish," he growled.

And pounced.

CHAPTER ELEVEN

When he sank into Nico's perfect heat again, Bas realized that although he'd thought he'd been in heaven before, he'd been completely wrong.

Because this? This contact, this closeness, this connection? *This* was heaven. And he never wanted to come back to earth.

Nico groaned beneath him. "I'm close. So close. I need... I need..."

"Shhh." Bas slid his arms under Nico's shoulders and lifted him, so Nico, still impaled on Bastien's cock, rested on Bas's thighs, his back to Bas's chest. "I've got you." He gripped Nico's cock and began to pump as he flexed his own hips.

Although Bas's own balls were tight, his own release teetering on the brink, Nico's pleasure was more important. No, not simply *important*. Nothing so trivial.

Vital.

As if only the expression of bliss that infused Nico's face when he came—as he had three times during the night as they'd alternately dozed and made love—was the key to Bas's own completion.

Then it happened. Nico shot over Bas's fist, the scent of musk and sweat like the sweetest perfume. And Bas fell over the brink—

And completely into love.

He cradled Nico's chest as he lowered them both to the bed, twisting at the last moment so they were on their sides and he didn't crush Nico as he pulled out and disposed of the condom.

"Mmmm." Nico hummed low in his throat and Bas laughed.

"You're purring just like Polita."

"Can you blame me?" Nico rolled to face Bas and pressed a kiss to the angle of his jaw. "You're very good at *petting* me. Even in places that can be a bit hard to reach."

Bas chuckled. "I'm glad my efforts have met with your approval." He touched his own face and grimaced. "Although I think I may need to invest in an industrial strength skin balm."

"Shea butter or aloe vera work well." He peered at Bas quizzically, probably because he couldn't focus clearly— they'd set his glasses aside after their first rather energetic fuck, lest they get broken. "Have you really never experienced beard burn before?" He propped himself up on an elbow, alarm chasing across his face as the dawn filtered in through a gap in the heavy velvet drapes. "Is it because you've never been with a man before? Because if that's the case, your superpower must be magical prostate location."

Bas lowered his chin and favored him with a sardonic glance. "Of course I've been with men before. Although I haven't been with anyone for quite some time." He gazed at Nico's concerned face. *What happens during the contract stays during the contract.*

But did he want it to stay? Or rather, did he want the contract to end? Nico was...*more*. More than Bas had expected. More than he'd realized. *More than I deserve.* He felt an overwhelming urge to give something back.

"That's not my power."

Nico tilted his head. "I was only joking."

"My power hasn't done anything more than keep my clothing unwrinkled and my brow sweat-free since I was a child. Never anything more." He smiled wryly. "Did you know that Corin was originally engaged as my valet when the man who'd served my father and then me decided to retire?"

Nico frowned. "No. He never told me. Only that he was going to be working for you at the New Palace." He shrugged apologetically. "We've been friends for years, but we both know how to be discreet on behalf of our employers."

Employers. God, that's what Bas was now. To Nico. *Sort of.* But he didn't want to be. He wanted to be more. He wanted Nico to be discreet on behalf of his lover. His fiancé. *His husband.* But if he wanted to color outside the lines of their agreement, Bas needed to be completely honest.

"Corin declared he didn't have enough to do as my valet. He proved that he could manage my rather convoluted personal affairs as well as my wardrobe without breaking a sweat of his own."

"Yes." Nico's voice sounded a little choked. "He's very efficient. And a master at delegating."

"But today…" Bas licked his lips, which were a trifle chapped after hours of kissing. "…today several things changed."

Nico's eyes widened and then his gaze flicked to the side. "Changed?"

"For one thing, as I mentioned, I've never gotten beard burn before. My rather limited deflection power has always saved my skin from any irritation."

"And blushes." Nico bit his lip. "Sorry. But I noticed that you blushed earlier. As far as I know—"

"I've never done that before either." Bas frowned. "Actually… Maybe I have. But only with Tarik. It's as if the deflection only works when it's concealing a vulnerability."

"So you don't mind being vulnerable with me?" Nico's smile was shy and so adorable that Bas had to kiss him again, chapped lips be damned.

"I suppose not." He settled Nico more comfortably against his chest. "Although the other thing, the other change was rather more...remarkable. That sculpture that fell in the hall of statues—"

"Thank goodness Medusa missed you. I'm still cross with you about that," Nico groused, but nestled closer, peering up at Bas with a cheeky grin. "I'm glad you've learned to obey me better since then."

Bas attempted to return the grin, but Tarik's words came back to him. Helena was here. She'd announced her intention of fulfilling the contract. Maybe that's what had activated his power. Nico was a commoner. He had no powers. *How can I keep him* and *the throne?*

He sighed. There really wasn't a choice. Anatole would make a terrible king, and the country—his people—would suffer.

"Medusa didn't miss me."

"What?" Nico reared back, his eyes wide. He scrabbled for his glasses on the bedside table and fumbled them on, one earpiece not seated correctly so they sat askew on his face. He mapped Bas's chest with his hands as though he were searching for hidden injuries. "Where? How— Why didn't you say something before I made you *exert* yourself like this?"

Bas caught Nico's wandering hand before it could investigate too far south and ignite his libido again. "I should be more precise. It did miss me, but only because it defied the laws of gravity and changed direction in midair." He kissed Nico's palm. "There was nobody there except Tarik and me, and his power is mental, not physical. My deflection power has increased. It's graduated from wrinkles and perspiration to several hundred pounds of cast iron."

Nico clenched his eyes shut. "Thank God."

"But, Nico, here's the thing. Tarik thinks it's because I've got a paired power."

"Paired power?"

Bas nodded. "It runs in my bloodline. My brother Crave found that his power increased after he met his Devin, and Devin's power increased as well. Louis IV"—he wet his lips —"had it too, with his first Queen. But when she died—"

"His power decreased," Nico murmured.

"Yes. We think that's why he cut such a wide swath through the female populace. Looking for another compatible power." Bas turned away, not wanting to face Nico when he announced the next thing. "When I met with Lady Helena earlier, before we made our agreement, she said she was prepared to take her place as my consort. I wouldn't have thought that would make a difference. We've never been precisely close. But there's no other way I can explain—"

"I can."

Am I really going to do this? Nico swallowed convulsively and ordered the butterflies battering his ribcage to settle down. If Bas believed that Lady Helena was the reason for his power surge, Nico had to give him all the facts.

Maybe Lady Helena *was* responsible. But as far as Nico knew—banishing snakes from the gardens notwithstanding —her powers hadn't altered.

Nico's had.

But if Nico revealed his own powers, he put every other powered commoner at risk, including Corin, most Municipal graduates, and—he suspected—Sander's valet Luken. Even if the hold-harmless clause in his fake engagement agreement with Bastien protected Nico (maybe), it could spawn some very awkward investigations. As he'd told Corin, a powered commoner's primary protection was anonymity.

Even for the greater good, though, he couldn't allow Bastien to commit himself to a marriage not of his own choosing.

Nico gazed fiercely into Bastien's eyes. "Don't do it. *Please* don't do it. You're a great king, regardless of your powers, and you deserve to be happy."

Bastien sighed. "I don't see any way around it. The new Minister of Powers isn't about to let me evade the Calibration Ceremony this time, and if marrying Helena will help me pass that test and keep Anatole off the throne —"

"No."

Bastien raised an eyebrow, a smile tugging at his lips. "Another command, my dear? I confess I won't say no, although given the time, I doubt I'll be able to give you the attention you deserve before we're interrupted by the obligations of the day."

"That's not what I—" Nico felt the flush rise through his chest and heat his cheeks. The notion of another chance at lovemaking with Bastien was almost more than he could resist, particularly since there was no guarantee they'd have another opportunity. He'd seen their schedules for the rest of Bonfire Fortnight. They'd barely have time to breathe, let alone sleep, and for some reason, they were always scheduled at separate events. He sat up despite Bastien's efforts to pull him against his chest. "Stop avoiding the Minister."

Bastien blinked at him. "What? But—"

"Have the Calibration Ceremony now. Today."

"Nico, I'm not sure—"

"Don't you get it?" Nico rolled to his knees, the sheets sliding off his thighs and making him shiver in the chill morning air. "If your powers are strong enough to deflect Medusa, they're strong enough to pass the test."

"Yeeesss. I know. That's why marrying Helena—"

"Don't be obtuse, *Your Majesty*. You don't need to marry her. You don't need to marry anyone you don't choose for any reason other than love. Once you pass the test, you'll never have to take it again. Your throne will be secure from that angle. And as long as we stay engaged until your birthday, you'll be safe there too."

Bastien frowned. "But if Louis is any indication, my powers will fade if I don't take Helena as my consort."

"So what?"

"I…beg your pardon?"

Nico bounced on his knees, jiggling the mattress. "So *what*? It won't matter, don't you see? You'll have already been certified. You'll never have to prove your power again. You've ruled well without powers until now. You can do it again. You don't have to flaunt your…your *prowess* in public. It's not really a public power, anyway."

"I suppose that's true, but—"

"Oh for God's sake, Bastien, do you *want* to be a martyr?"

Bastien's lips twitched. "It's not my preferred path, no."

"Then get this stupid test over with and get on with your life. As soon as we—" Nico swallowed against a lump in his throat. "—terminate our engagement, you'll be completely free to find a consort of your own choosing in your own time." He dropped his gaze to his lap. "Nobody should be deprived of that. Not even a king."

Bastien's eyes had widened as Nico spoke. "Oh my God. That's brilliant." He sat up, but only long enough to pull Nico back down against him, chest to chest, hip to hip, cock to cock. "You're brilliant. No wonder Tarik thinks the world of you."

But do you *think the world of me?* As Bastien kissed him soundly, Nico couldn't vanquish the vain hope that Bastien returned his regard. Even as Bastien entered him again—*I'm going to feel him for days*—Nico tried to remind himself that this wouldn't last. Wishing for more was ludicrous. Because the whole point of the fake engagement was for Bastien to be allowed to choose for himself.

And why would the king, who could have anybody, ever choose me?

CHAPTER TWELVE

Although the sunlight was strengthening in the gap between the drapes, the bedroom was still dark enough that Bas could pretend the night wasn't over. He'd barely slept and ought to be exhausted, but his time with Nico had somehow energized him.

And Nico had once again found a way to release Bas from chains not of his own making. The man was a bloody miracle. *What momentous changes could he kindle if he truly were the King Consort?*

Didn't his people deserve that kind of advocate? Somebody not steeped in generations of antiquated traditions and dusty protocols? An out-of-the-box thinker who'd challenge the old guard every day and champion the commoners in the way so many Royals neglected to do, despite noblesse oblige.

If I refuse to break our contract—

Bastien clenched his eyes shut and huffed a breath. Trapping Nico into marriage wouldn't be any different from the snare he'd helped Bas escape. Besides, Nico and Corin had worded that contract to ensure Nico had a valid exit strategy. Bas *couldn't* haul him to the altar and solemnize the damned match, no matter how much he wanted to.

But he was tempted. *God*, he was tempted. Perhaps he could court Nico in earnest once they were officially ex-fiancés. It would be unusual, but wouldn't people view it as romantic? *Unless they view it as another attempt by a Royal to impose his own passions on an unwilling victim.*

If Bas had even a breath of a hope of something between them in the future, something permanent, he needed to let Nico know what he faced.

Nico's gaze was so clear. So trusting. So accepting and nonjudgmental that Bas could admit his deepest fear. Confess something he'd never said even to Tarik, his closest friend. "Do you know," he said, shifting his gaze from Nico's eyes to where his hand rested on Nico's bare hip, "that the Y chromosome doesn't change?"

"So we're talking about genetics now?" Nico's tone was playful, but tinged with uncertainty. *As it should be, considering this enormous non sequitur.*

"Yes. Recombinant DNA, the engine of human diversity, the centrifuge that spawned the possibility for powers in the Abarran hills so long ago."

"All right." Nico kissed Bas's shoulder. "I admit I paid more attention to my contract law classes than biology when I was in school, but I'm listening."

"For someone assigned female at birth, the twenty-third chromosomal pair has two X chromosomes, one from the father and one from the mother. X chromosomes recombine, so genes could change, be expressed differently through inheritance. But for male-assigned, that pair has an X and a Y. And the Y chromosome does not recombine. Your Y chromosome is exactly the same as your father's, his the same as his father's, and so on back up the ancestry chain. Always the same, barring any mutations or damage. Although those mutations and damage are then replicated going forward."

"Interesting, Bastien, but is there a reason—"

"Yes." He closed his eyes and took a breath. "Sorry. I don't mean to be autocratic."

Nico stroked his cheek. "You're not. Go on."

"Unlike South Abarra, where, like now, the monarchy passed from father to daughter or from mother to daughter as well as from father to son, the kingship in North Abarra is an unbroken father-to-son male line going back to the Schism."

"Okay."

From Nico's puzzled tone, he still didn't understand what Bas was trying, apparently unsuccessfully, to point out. "That means there's a part of me, that bloody Y chromosome, that's exactly the same as my father, as his father." He swallowed. "As Louis IV."

"Hold it." Nico frowned and pushed up on one elbow to stare down at Bas.

I knew it. He's revolted. Once he realizes what that means— He steeled himself, wanting to remember the last sight of Nico's skin, the last touch of his hand, the last whisper of his breath across Bas's cheek. *I might be able to deflect a cast iron Medusa, but this blow will level me.*

"Bastien, do you *seriously* believe you're the same as your father? As the Mad King?" Was that anger in Nico's tone? Revulsion? Contempt?

Bas closed his eyes, so he wouldn't see the accusation dawn in Nico's eyes, the same fury that infused the faces of protesters, the mobs that decried him as *King Bastard*. "I am the same. It's there, Nico. Baked into every cell in my body."

The bedclothes rustled. *He's leaving.* Bas rolled onto his back and flung his arm over his eyes, the better to block out the sight. *Maybe I can ask housekeeping to save these sheets, so I'll still have his scent.*

"Bastien."

"You can go."

"Bastien."

"I'll make sure you—"

"*Bastien*. Look at me."

"Do I have to?" Bas croaked, his throat constricted.

"Yes."

Bas sighed and lowered his arm, but waited another interminable three seconds before he opened his eyes. Nico was leaning on one arm, his torso blocking the dim light filtering in through the drapes so Bas couldn't make out his face. "I'm looking."

"Looking isn't the same as seeing."

"Well, it's bloody dark! What do you expect?"

"I expect you to listen to what I'm about to say. Listen very carefully."

As little as Bas wanted to hear the same recriminations in Nico's voice as he heard daily from Parliament, from disaffected Royals, from the conservative press, he owed it to Nico to let him have his say. "All right."

"In the first place, I can't go. We're in my bedroom."

Bas blinked at him. "Oh. Right." Bas tossed off the sheets. "I'll—"

"Hold it right there." Nico slapped a hand in the middle of Bas's chest and pushed him back onto the pillows. "I'm not done."

"All right. Please. Go on." *Especially if you keep touching me.*

"You"—Nico said, glaring into Bas's eyes—"are not your father. You are not the Mad King."

"But the possibility is there, the potential, the risk—"

"Bullshit. There's more to you than a fricking Y chromosome." Nico brushed Bas's hair off his forehead—somehow, it was only ever tousled in Nico's presence, possibly because Bas's inner supo craved that gesture, that tender touch. "Your mind." He touched Bas's chest. "Your heart." He rested his hand on Bas's belly. "Your strength. Your education and training and principles. You're *you*. There's never been anybody like you, and there never will be again. You choose to be good. And because you choose it, you *are* good.

"Thank you," Bas croaked. "I'm so happy you think so, because—"

A knock sounded on the bedroom door. "Your Majesty? Your breakfast is ready in your sitting room," Rozenn said, her voice muffled by the thick oak panels.

"Thank you, Baroness." He smiled at Nico, his heart lighter than it had been in years. "Interesting that she knew where to find me."

"I suspect Gaston and Pascal might have given her a hint," Nico said dryly.

Bas laughed. "A point. Ah well, it appears we can no longer avoid the day. Eat with me?"

Nico smiled. "Of course." He glanced down at his body, which was painted with the evidence of their last round. "Although perhaps I should shower first or the stench will interfere with the aroma of the pastries."

"You smell divine." Bastien grinned. "But you're welcome to share the shower with me." He widened his eyes in mock innocence at Nico's narrow-eyed glance. "It's the most efficient use of time, and I know you're a stalwart champion of efficiency."

"Uh huh."

As it happened, Bas was *very* efficient when he sucked Nico off amid the steam with the water pounding hot on his back.

Nico tugged on the hem of the green jacket, even though it wasn't necessary. The thing fit perfectly, as did the black trousers and the shiny black oxfords. The outfit—along with one of Bastien's—had appeared in his dressing room at some point between yesterday evening and this morning's shower. Nico pulled at the high collar. It was completely comfortable, but he didn't really want to think about what whoever delivered the uniform—*not Corin, please not Corin*—had heard through the bedroom door.

Bastien emerged from the dressing room, Polita riding on his shoulder. His jacket was the same high-collared, double-breasted cut, with the same gold buttons as Nico's but decorated with his usual raft of medals and gold bullion. Nico's was plainer, although the gold sash—*like a freaking beauty pageant contestant*—added a little too much bling for Nico's liking.

Bastien raised both eyebrows as he took in Nico. "You're very handsome in your uniform." He waggled his eyebrows. "It makes me want to strip you out of it."

Nico flushed, mortified that his cock twitched. After Bastien took him down the royal throat in the shower, Nico had been certain it wouldn't be able to rise for another week. "Um...thank you. You look nice too." He mentally rolled his eyes. Talk about an understatement. Bastien looked perfect, as always.

Bastien strolled over to the table with its silver-domed plates and three-tiered tea tray. Nico peered at him as he passed. "Why don't you have cat fur all over your jacket?"

Bastien shot Nico a devastating grin as he transferred Polita to the sofa, then sat at the table and snapped his linen napkin with a flourish before arranging it across his lap. He selected a scone from the tray. "Have you forgotten that deflecting harmful things is apparently my superpower?"

Nico scowled as he sat opposite him and arranged his own napkin. "I'd hardly call cat fur *harmful*."

"Ah, but it's harmful to my reputation as the always-dapper king who never lets anything—from fractious MPs to over-warm weather to ill-behaved kittens—ruffle my sangfroid." He grasped the handle of the teapot. "Shall I pour?"

"I can—"

"I know," Bastien said softly. "But I want to. I find that I rather enjoy caring for my fiancé." His smile turned a little wicked. "In any number of ways."

Okay, now Nico was certain his blush would set off the Palace smoke detectors. "Th-thank you." As soon as Bastien filled Nico's cup, he snatched it up and took a gulp.

"Careful!" Bastien set the pot down with a clatter. "You'll scald your mouth."

Nico shook his head. "I'm fine." The tea was hot, true. *Very* hot, but his failure to doctor it with a little honey was the problem more than its heat.

"Very well." Bastien gave him a sheepish glance. "I hope you'll forgive me for reading at the breakfast table, but I need to go over my schedule for the day or Corin will have my head."

Nico chuckled. "Mine too. He showed me my appointments last night. Apparently I've suddenly become very popular with a number of people who'd never acknowledged my existence before."

Bastien grimaced. "Yes. I'm afraid that's a drawback we didn't fully discuss before you signed on to be…"

"Your ex?" Nico kept his tone light, but for some reason Bastien didn't smile. "It's all right. I assumed there would be responsibilities attached." He glanced at the cream linen card next to his plate, his schedule inscribed in beautiful copperplate calligraphy. "Although I admit I expected we'd be spending at least *some* time together. According to this, we'll be lucky if we're in the same room again between now and Bonfire Night."

Bastien's eyes twinkled over the rim of his teacup. "Believe me, that won't stand, not if I have to rearrange the agenda myself." He lifted his chin, his lips tilting down at the corners in an expression of mock superiority. "I'm the king. I can do that, you know."

Nico chuckled. "I'd heard."

"At the very least, I'll want you at the Calibration Ceremony. Oh!" He ate a last bite of his scone. "I should let Corin know to arrange that with the Minister. Today, I think you said?" He glanced down at his own schedule, which didn't look any less dense than Nico's. "Maybe— Blast!" He crumpled his napkin in his fist and stood up. "I forgot. I arranged to meet with Lady Helena this morning. She'll be arriving any moment."

Nico struggled out of his chair too. "Here?"

"No. Nothing so dire. My office in the governmental wing. But I'll need to hurry if I expect to be there when she arrives. Although I can send Gaston on ahead in case she's early."

The door to Bastien's office. A broad back in a guard uniform. A hefty stick held over a shoulder. A cry as the stick comes down and up. Down and up. Down and up.

"Nico?" Bastien's voice. His hands gripping Nico's arms.

Nico sucked in a breath. *He's here. We're here. He's all right.* "Don't go."

"What? Nico, I have to face her in person. Apologize for any misconceptions she might have for this invitation. Surely you see that?"

That's not what I see. "Please, Bastien. Don't go. And Gaston. Don't… Ask for someone else. Pascal. Marco. One of the others. Not Gaston."

Bastien's eyes narrowed, and he dropped his hands. "It's not Helena who activated my powers, is it?"

"Please," Nico whimpered. "I can't."

Bastien advanced on him, his eyes nearly black. "When were you going to confess, Nico? When were you going to tell me you have powers too?"

CHAPTER THIRTEEN

"You have powers too."

Nico's head reeled. This couldn't be happening. His life, Corin's life, every powered commoner's life was on the line unless he could convince Bastien to let this go. But how could he? When he saw Gaston beating the king to death?

And the king. He looked so...intense. Angry? Of course. How could he not be? Nico had been hiding a capital offense from him, from Tarik, from everyone in the palace, since the moment they'd met.

Nico snatched his hands behind his back, as if hiding them would somehow conceal the truth. "I... I..."

Bastien advanced on him, as lethal as a panther. "Tell me, Nico. Why don't you want me to go? Why don't you want me to take Gaston, the captain of my guard, the man whom I spar with privately several times a week? Why?"

But as loath as Nico was to reveal his secrets, he wouldn't, he *couldn't* let anything happen to Bastien, even if it meant Bastien hated him for his subterfuge. *Jail will be easier.*

"I saw him."

Bastien edged closer, eyes narrowed. "Saw him where? Out the window? Did you open the door when I was dressing? How?"

"No." Nico tapped his temple. "In here."

"You'll have to do better than that. I'm not about to accuse one of my most trusted allies on the basis of your imagination."

Anger sparked in Nico's belly, giving him the approximation of a spine. "It's *not* my imagination. I have... visions. Foresight. It's limited, but it's been changing lately, and I—"

"Changing?" Bas grasped Nico's arms again, but immediately released him at Nico's wince. "Your powers are changing too? Getting stronger?"

Nico nodded miserably. "Yes. But—"

"You know what this means?" Was that elation in Bastien's voice? He was grinning almost maniacally. "*You're* my paired power. *You're* my perfect match."

"We don't know that for sure," Nico said weakly.

"My powers have grown. Yours have too. *Of course* we know for sure." Bastien threw back his head and laughed.

"Well, it's not that funny," Nico said testily. "If anyone finds out, I'll get tossed in prison. Commoners aren't allowed to have powers."

Bastien snorted, but began pacing across the carpet, much to Polita's disapproval. "Just because they're not legally recognized doesn't mean they don't exist." He spun to face Nico. "You've got Royal blood. Somewhere in your ancestry, you've got Royal blood."

Nico shook his head. "I don't."

"You can't know that. Royals in both countries were incapable of discretion when it came to indulging their sexual appetites. Even if your bloodline was one of the discontinued ones, the disavowed, it's still allowable under the law. All we need to do is trace it back. The Municipal has testing protocols. The Ministry—"

"I've *been* tested, Bastien. And I don't conform to any of the recorded bloodlines. I'm a fluke. A freak. And if you tell anyone about me, it means the end of my life as a free man."

And possibly the end of others' freedom, too, should Bastien reveal the information to the hardliners at the Ministry.

Bastien, incredibly enough, waved a hand as if batting Nico's words, his concerns, his terror, away like cobwebs. "Ah, but that's where you're wrong. As soon as we're married, you're legally Royal." He spread his hands as if he'd just pulled a rabbit out of his hat. "Problem solved."

Nico shook his head slowly. "The result is the same, Bastien. It's still the end of my life as a free man."

Bastien inhaled sharply, as if he'd been punched in the gut. "I...see." He let his breath out slowly, shoulders sinking, medals *clink*ing. "You have no desire to be bound beyond our agreement." His smile was crooked and regretful and nearly broke Nico's heart. "You signed on to be the king's ex. You made that perfectly clear."

"It's not that," Nico croaked, although he wasn't sure Bastien heard him.

"Then what is it?" Bastien demanded.

"Louis," Nico whispered.

Bastien stared at him, and again, Nico saw what nobody else had ever seen: the king as pale as death. "Louis."

"If you marry me so you don't lose your powers, you're —"

"Doing exactly what Louis did." Bastien's shoulders sagged. "I'm sorry. That's exactly what it looks like. But Nico—" A knock sounded on the door, and Bastien cursed under his breath. "What is it?" he barked.

"Your Majesty," Corin called, "Lady Helena is awaiting you in your office."

"Blast," he muttered, but then his eyes widened. "What did you see, Nico? Your vision? What exactly did you see? Quickly! We might already be too late."

"Y-your office door. Gaston's back."

"You're sure it was Gaston?"

"I recognize his hair. None of the other guards is ginger. Plus, he had the captain's epaulettes on his shoulders."

"All right. What was he doing?"

"He was holding a thick wooden stick, about five or six feet long."

"His quarterstaff," Bastien murmured. "We were supposed to spar this morning."

"He raised it and brought it down. Hard. Multiple times."

Bastien licked his lips. "Did you see his...his victim?"

"No. He was blocking my view. But the vision hit me when you said you were going to meet Lady Helena with Gaston. My visions are always referential. Triggered by a comment or a question." *If-this-then-that.*

Bastien pointed at him. "You stay here. If what I'm afraid of is happening, Gaston may be murdering Helena as we speak, and as little as I want to marry her, I don't want her dead either."

"Bastien, wait!" Nico grabbed Bas's arm as he lunged toward the door. "You're playing into my vision."

"I know. I have to stop Gaston."

"No, don't you see?" Nico said, his tone desperate. "If you go, that's exactly the scenario that will play out. You won't stop it. You'll be part of it."

Bas scowled. "What are you talking about? What good is a vision if you can't do anything about it?"

Nico scowled back. "You think I haven't asked that question? I haven't gotten a handle on the way my power has changed, but before it was always cautionary. I'd get a vision of something that was needed to prevent a problem. Small things. Like a pen so Tarik could sign a contract. Or the corkscrew that he forgot for the tasting ceremony. But now, I'm seeing a bigger picture—Medusa falling, for instance. Something that will happen if a particular choice is made, a specific path is taken. It's...it's like *if-this-then-that*. Cause and effect. You walked down the hall of statues—"

"And Medusa fell," Bas muttered. "You're saying it was an intentional attempt on my life?"

"Of course it was! Corin said it took six men to position the thing in the first place. It couldn't just tip over unless it was *engineered* to tip over."

"Or it was the result of supo intervention."

Nico nodded. "That wasn't the first time. When...when I took your arm before the progress to the Sequestrium. Well, you'd just asked if I was sure, if I was ready. Taking your arm was my choice to continue, and that's when I saw it." His face paled. "The crash. The breaking glass. The chanting."

"You saw the attack? Why didn't you say something?"

"What? 'Oh, pardon me, Your Majesty, while I freak out about a random hallucination?'" Nico said tartly. "It had never happened before!"

Bas ran his hands through his hair. "I'm sorry. Of course, if it's a recent change, you wouldn't have known. So that, the hall of statues, and Gaston's attack. Have there been any others?"

Nico blushed, pink tinting the crests of his cheekbones. "There was one other. But it was...um...personal." He seemed to shake off his embarrassment. "But I was able to try something with it. An...an A-B test, if you will. I chose B, and result B followed."

Bas studied Nico's earnest face. He truly believed what he was saying. Could Bas really contradict him? His own changing powers were evidence that reality was more fluid than it appeared, particularly when it came to Royal—or apparently commoner—powers. "All right. What do you suggest?"

Nico frowned, his brows dipping below the edge of his glasses. "There are two things that need to happen without your presence. Lady Helena should be intercepted and taken to a place of safety, and Gaston should be detained elsewhere." He glared at Bas. "And not by you."

"I can hardly arrest the man for no reason. He's captain of the guard, for God's sake."

"And you're the king. Please, Bastien. Do it."

Although Bas's instinct was still to rush into the fray, to see if events really would play out as Nico claimed, he nodded. "Very well. But I don't want this made public. Not until we know the truth."

Nico hesitated, but then said, "All right."

Keeping his gaze fixed on Nico, Bas retrieved his specially configured cell phone—the one that only communicated with Tarik on their special frequency—from his jacket pocket. "I trust Tarik with my life. Let's just hope he isn't lolling in his enormous bathtub or indulging in a round of leisurely morning sex with Sander. Or both." But when he touched the emergency dial icon, Tarik answered almost immediately.

"Bas. I'm in your office. Where the fuck are you?"

"Still in my quarters. Why?"

"Because Ferran Rey has gathered a posse of his fellow reactionary MPs and they're marching through the halls toward—"

"Not my office," Bas said, alarm pooling in his belly.

"No. Isabel's. Apparently they intend to lodge a complaint with her and demand she reconvene Parliament to force you to honor the original betrothal contract."

Bas pinched the bridge of his nose. "I should have known he wouldn't take this lying down. Is the Duchess involved too? Lady Helena?"

"No. The Duchess is with your mother, who… Sorry, Bas, but your mother still believes that the wedding will be between you and Helena. She keeps referring to Helena as your fiancée and enthusing about the wedding breakfast arrangements. Rozenn is looking extremely frazzled, which I don't think has ever happened. She's ordinarily more unflappable than you."

"Is Helena with them?"

"No. I think she's on her way here, since you have an appointment scheduled." Tarik's tone—as acerbic mentally as it was physically—turned irritated. "Which, I hope, is intended to be you apologizing to her and wishing her a nice life and not you apologizing to her and asking her to accept your rather fickle hand in marriage."

"I—"

"Don't give in to them, Bas. Not Ferran and his bullies. Not your mother and her rather addled dreams. Nico is good for you. Helena isn't. Although"—his voice took on a speculative tone—"to be fair, I don't think she's buying in to either her father's or your mother's plans. She called here a minute ago to make sure you'd be here, and sounded apologetic and a little worried. I sent Gaston to escort her from her—"

"What?" Bas's grip on the phone tightened, its edges biting into his palm. "Belay that order. In fact, have somebody grab Gaston and restrain him."

"Gaston? Who the fuck could restrain *him*? He's as big as a house."

"Ten somebodies, then. And have somebody else—you and Sander, if you can't find anybody else you trust—bring Helena to my private sitting room."

"What—"

"Later, Tarik. I'll explain everything later."

Tarik sighed. "Whatever you say. But I'll hold your feet to the fire until you make good on that."

Bas tucked the phone back into his pocket. "There. Different choices made. But I really do need to head to my office now. Is that all right?"

Nico's eyes glazed over, but then a smile trembled on his lips. "Yes. You'll be okay. I see you laughing with Princess Katalin now."

"If Kat's back, she can take charge of this menace." He scooped Polita up from where she'd been pouncing on his shoelaces and handed her to Nico. But when Nico would have stepped back, Bas gripped his wrist gently and pulled him close enough to drop a soft kiss on his forehead. "I know I'm asking a lot. But would you please wait in my sitting room with Helena? After we're sure she's safe, we have things to discuss."

Nico gulped, but nodded, cuddling a purring Polita to his chest. "All right."

"Good." Bas straightened his shoulders and strode out of the room, nodding at Pascal on his way past. He made a mental note to increase the guard contingent in the corridor —because if political unrest had gone far enough to compromise Gaston, of all people, then nobody in the palace was safe.

Nico stood next to the window in Bastien's study, cradling Polita, and stared at the stone walls that enclosed the palace grounds. Were the crowds still out there, still angry? Through the thick windows—bulletproof glass, Corin had told him—he couldn't hear any shouts or chanting. He was tempted to open the french doors and step out onto the balcony, if only so he could catch his breath. The spacious room seemed close and airless, and every breath seemed to stall halfway down his lungs.

Bastien knew the truth about Nico now. But Nico wasn't certain whether he was angry or...sensing an opportunity.

He'd told Bastien that he wasn't Louis, but really, Bastien had never had any reason to *be* like Louis.

Now he did.

If Bastien refused to honor the terms of their agreement, if he didn't break the engagement after Bonfire Fortnight, what recourse did Nico have? Bastien was the king. Nico was nobody. No, scratch that. Nico was a commoner with illegal powers, and if the king wanted to exploit those for himself, all he had to do was threaten to expose Nico to the Ministry. One swipe of their calibration meters would be enough to convict him.

So—marriage to a gorgeous, powerful man who made love like a dream but didn't love him, or life in prison? Both were prisons of a sort, although one cage was significantly more gilded than the other.

Nico wasn't stupid. He knew which one he'd choose if Bastien gave him an ultimatum.

But he wished—with all his heart, he wished—that Bastien wouldn't make that demand. Because if Bastien turned out to be no better than any other selfish, entitled Royal rather than the principled king who tried always to do the right thing, it would break Nico's heart.

As if walking away from him at the end of the contract won't do the same.

He scratched the kitten behind her ears. "How stupid am I for falling in love with my fake fiancé? Isn't that some kind of romance novel cliche?" He sighed. "What am I going to do, Polita?" Polita apparently had no insight, because she struggled out of his arms and dashed under the sofa. "Thanks so much for your help."

He turned back to the scene out the windows. Some of the grounds staff were peering worriedly into the fire pit. Was the snake incursion still going on?

The door opened behind him and he swung around. Lady Helena stood in the doorway, her beaded peach silk cocktail gown and matching stilettos perhaps a bit elaborate for morning wear. She was speaking, low and somewhat intensely, to someone outside in the corridor. Nico rubbed his damp palms on his trousers, the high-end wool soft and smooth under his hands as his usual suits were not.

What did you say to the king's ex when you were her unexpected replacement? Pretend you didn't know anything about the betrothal contract? That would be pretty disingenuous, considering the contents were public knowledge. Should he apologize?

Nico tested those two choices, nudging his power to see if it would actually respond to his command rather than acting on its own chaotic agenda.

But he got nothing.

Did that mean his power was being its usual diva self, or that either path would produce the same result? Damn it, he wished he had more time to test this on less life-altering choices. Like whether a change in the Royal Crest labeling would boost their sagging US sales. Or whether Polita preferred the chicken or fish cat food.

One way or another, this was bound to be awkward. So he waited by the window until Lady Helena allowed Pascal to close the door behind her. Her glance swept the room. Nico frowned, because she didn't look alarmed or relieved or hesitant.

She looked triumphant.

Her gaze passed over him twice without registering his presence. He supposed that in his forest green uniform, standing against the forest green drapes, he might be somewhat camouflaged. But he wasn't *invisible*, for God's sake.

He cleared his throat, and she startled. "Oh!" Her expression altered to something slightly more neutral. "You're here."

"Yes." Nico decided not to elaborate. After all, it was pretty obvious.

"I believe Bastien wanted to speak to me privately." She advanced into the room and sat gracefully on the loveseat rather than in one of the armchairs, the obvious insinuation that Bastien would be sitting beside her when he arrived. "I'd like a bit of time to compose myself." Her smile was calculated to be brave and self-deprecating, but for some reason, it struck Nico as false. "I'm sure you understand."

"Go right ahead. There's tea, if you'd like some. It should still be hot."

A wrinkle marred the white skin of her forehead. "I'd like to be alone until the king arrives."

Nico offered her a strained smile as a low throb of pain began thrumming behind his left eye. *Great*. Was his power going to be like Tarik's? Giving him headaches whenever he tried to use it? "That's understandable."

The wrinkle deepened, her mouth turning down. "Yet apparently *you* don't understand. I'd like you to leave. Consider this a polite request."

Nico blinked, the pain spiking a little higher. She didn't sound particularly polite. In fact, she sounded downright peevish. "Noted. However, Bastien asked me to wait here. So I intend to wait. If he wants me to leave once he gets back, I'll be glad to comply."

Her eyes narrowed, and now she didn't look peevish so much as murderous. *Guess she's not as accepting of Bastien's announcement as she seemed*. "If I have to, I'll call the guard to escort you."

He shrugged. "You can certainly try. However, since he's my guard, he'll probably do as I ask, and as Bastien ordered him before he left."

Her smile made Nico shiver. She was supposed to be a famously serene beauty, but that smile was as cruel as any he'd ever seen. "We'll see about that." She leaned back in the loveseat and crossed her legs, idly swinging her foot in its red-soled stiletto. *That color really doesn't go well with peach.* "Guard," she called, not bothering to look away from the flames dancing in the fireplace.

Pascal opened the door and stood at attention on the threshold. "Yes, Your Majesty."

Your Majesty? WTF?

Still not glancing at Pascal, she flicked her fingers in Nico's direction. "This commoner has intruded on my personal quarters. Please have him taken to the dungeons immediately. I'm sure the king will announce his arrest and incarceration any moment now."

"Yes, Your Majesty."

Pascal advanced toward Nico, his heavy boots soundless on the plush carpet, his expression not so much stoic as blank. "Come quietly and it will go easier for you."

Nico backed up, the velvet drapes heavy against his back. "Pascal. It's me." Pascal kept coming—and Lady Helena's smile grew. Nico was practically wearing the drapes now. "Pascal. Stop!"

Pascal didn't stop. But he blinked, then squinted as if he were trying to make something out with a bright light shining in his eyes. Then his face went blank again.

He veered to the right and stood with his nose pressed against the window, unmoving.

Nico peered at him, although he didn't emerge from his velvet cocoon. Pascal didn't appear to register that he was imitating a kid at a bakery store window. It was as if he'd just…switched off, like a toy whose battery had run out.

"Guard!" Lady Helena's voice was sharp, commanding, nothing like the wan tones she'd affected when she arrived. "Guard, do as I say. Arrest this pretender. Protect your future Queen. Protect your King."

Nico edged away, even though Pascal didn't seem to be paying attention. He stood behind the chair—Bastien's favorite—and stared somberly at Lady Helena. Maybe she was under a misapprehension about her appointment with Bastien today. Understandable, since Bastien had intended to confer just such an honor on her until Nico showed him a way out.

"I'm sorry, my lady, but you're not the future Queen. I know it probably came as a bit of a shock—"

"Shut up," she said, baring her teeth.

The pain bloomed behind his eye again. *Not using my powers again until I've stockpiled ibuprofen.* "You probably expected a different message from Bastien this morning, especially when you were escorted here—"

"I told you to *shut up*." Spittle flew from her perfect red lips, which didn't look quite so perfect now. Rather thin and pinched, as a matter of fact.

Another throb made Nico massage his temple. He could make allowances for someone who'd sustained such a significant disappointment. He'd had loads of experience terminating employees for unsatisfactory performance and handling temperamental customers. Surely he could manage one irritated Royal for a few minutes, especially since Lady Helena's reptile communication power wasn't really threat here. Not unless snakes could crawl up two stories' worth of sandstone.

Er...can they? Nico pushed that alarming thought aside and tried the smile that had disarmed many an irate supplier. "I heard you. If you don't mind my saying so, it wasn't particularly polite, and not in keeping with your public reputation, but I can make allowances under the circumstances. You've sustained a disappointment. But since you and Bastien haven't committed to one another and aren't in love—"

"Love?" she scoffed. "As if I could ever love that piece of Northern shit."

Nico's jaw dropped. "What—"

"I don't know what is going on here. Why are you refusing to do as you're told?"

"Maybe because you've got no authority over me?"

Her lip lifted in a sneer. "Discrediting you would have been neater." She rose, a silver knife flashing in her fist. *Where did she get that?* "I dislike getting blood on my hands, but needs must." She circled the marble table, tapping the knife against her skirt. "How shocking that the upstart who bewitched the king also attacked his consort. What a blessing that she was able to fight him off."

Nico sidestepped, keeping the chair between them. "Did you just refer to yourself in the third person?"

She waved his words away—with the tip of the knife. "I make it a practice to rehearse my sound bites," she said matter-of-factly. "They're easier to insert into the appropriate minds that way."

Nico froze, his hands clutching the chair back. *Insert into...* "You. You're...Mastermind?"

Her smile was brilliant, as if she was flattered by the accusation. "Do you know how irritating it is to have other people credited with my work? Necessary, but so disheartening." She tilted her head, gazing at him with what looked like real affection. "Recognition is so gratifying. I'd almost be tempted to let you live, except for some reason, you're resistant. I've never run into anybody else who was this resistant, except, for some exasperating reason, Bastien. But as long as everybody else bows to my will, it won't matter what he says. In fact, they'll probably lock him up all the sooner for being a raving lunatic, leaving his poor bereaved Queen Consort to act as regent for their unborn child."

Somewhere amid his horror at her announcement, Nico found space to be doubly horrified by the notion she might be... "You're pregnant?"

"Not yet. But it's only a matter of time. I'll take care of it at *our* Sequester. If my powers won't affect him, I'm certain the correct dosage of Rohypnol will do the trick."

CHAPTER FOURTEEN

The private corridors were empty as Bas practically ran through them. Ordinarily, he liked to keep to the public hallways, wanting the staff, family, and guests to see him as an accessible king.

Not today. Today was about speed and efficiency. Today was about saving his damn kingdom.

He burst through the door into the governmental wing and practically ran full-tilt into Tarik.

"About time you got here," Tarik growled, grabbing Bas's elbow and towing him toward where a gaggle of guards milled about outside his office. "Come on."

"You may release your viselike grip. I have no intention of resisting, since you're heading in precisely the direction I wish. But—"

"Stop talking." Tarik didn't release Bas's arm and didn't slow down. "Just stop."

Given his cousin's fierce scowl, Bas decided arguing for the sake of having the last word was ill-advised. But as they neared two somber guards who were standing rather randomly in the center of the hall between his office door and a small audience chamber, something fizzled along Bas's skin as if he'd been dunked in a pool of static.

Tarik released his arm and heaved an audible sigh. "Thank fuck."

Bas rubbed his chest, his heart resuming its normal rhythm. "What was that?"

Tarik nodded to the guards and jerked his head toward the office. "Sander's inside. He's maintaining a magnetic field within your office and in this section of the palace, but he can't extend his range without exhausting himself."

"Why does he..." Bas's voice trailed off as he passed the two guards—neither of them Gaston—flanking his office door. Sander was standing next to the window, his fists clenched as he held them in front of his body. Bas recognized the pose—he'd seen it at the wedding when Sander had taken out all the mechanical systems in the Dulibre Festival Hall to rescue Tarik.

A frowning Katalin was sitting on Bas's desk, swinging her booted feet, and shedding mud and dust all over his rug. Her face cleared when she saw him. "Bas!"

She leaped off and raced across the room to hug him. "Thank goodness you're okay."

He hugged her back, and some inner instinct that he'd never noticed until now kicked in and he intentionally deflected the dust and mud from his person—and Kat's too, although the cleaning staff might have words with him about the mess on the carpet. "Of course I am. Why wouldn't I be?"

Tarik hurried over to Sander. "You okay, babe?"

Sander smiled tightly, and Bas noticed that perspiration was standing out on his forehead under the fall of his brown hair. "Fine. But let me concentrate?"

Bas peered down at Katalin. "He's not blowing out all the electronics in the New Palace, is he? Because that could make the Crown's Chamberlain extremely cross."

Katalin shivered. "Brrr. Nobody wants the Baroness mad at them."

With one final stroke to Sander's back, Tarik crossed to Bas. "Don't be insulting. He's got more control than that. He's maintaining a protective magnetic bubble."

Bas raised his eyebrows. "You're experiencing that much airwave chatter?"

Tarik's mouth flattened in a grim line. "It blocks more than just transmission frequencies. Think about it. Brainwaves are electrical impulses too. He's keeping everyone inside this bubble free of mind control influence."

Bas's knees threatened to buckle. "Mastermind?"

Tarik nodded. "It took six guards to take down Gaston, him hollering about treason and pretenders to the throne and I don't know what all else. They tossed him in one of the supo containment cells because it was closest, and as soon as he was behind the negation bars, he snapped out of it. Didn't know where he was, demanding to know where you were, accusing his lieutenants of treason. Yada yada yada."

"You're sure?"

Tarik gave him a *seriously?* look. "Of anybody in the New Palace, I know what it's like having Mastermind take a joy ride in your brain. He can put whatever he wants in there— sights, smells, sounds, it all feels real. But while he can put shit in, he can't take shit out. If he could, he'd have done a better job characterizing you and Sander's bitchy cousin."

Bas lifted an eyebrow. "The password."

"Exactly. Mastermind can control thoughts, but he can't read minds. When Gaston couldn't give the password, the lieutenants didn't hesitate."

"And you're sure Mastermind can't penetrate Sander's magnetic shield?"

Tarik glared at him disgustedly. "There you go with the insults again."

Bas sank onto the loveseat. "Thank goodness you got Lady Helena away first." *Thank goodness Nico wasn't here.*

"It wasn't easy," Tarik said, dropping into the opposite armchair and propping his elbows on his knees. "She was out in the gardens again, convincing yet another snake that it really shouldn't attack Bonfire Night revelers." He chuckled. "As I understand it, snakes have their own political agenda and were advocating for a greater rodent population in the gardens."

Katalin frowned. "Is that what she said?"

"Yeah." Tarik leaned against the wall, arms crossed. "She says they've been alarmed by the gardeners' success in ground squirrel reduction."

Katalin clutched Bas's sleeve. "That's not what they're saying."

The hair on Bas's neck stood at attention. "The snakes?"

"I had to rescue a couple of them on my way in. They're practically catatonic, they're so upset. Somebody is forcing them to leave their secure nests and come here."

Tarik blanched. "Mastermind can control snakes?"

Bas shared a horrified glance with Tarik. "If that's not what the snakes are saying but Helena claims that they are…"

"But…but…" Tarik ran a shaking hand through his hair. "She's been helping the groundskeepers. Convincing the snakes to leave."

"Convincing, bullshit," Katalin said. "They were desperate to get away. Somebody's been keeping them here."

Tarik and Bas exchanged a horrified glance. *"Helena?* Helena is Mastermind?"

"Fuck," Tarik muttered.

Bas's belly filled with ice and he jumped up. "Nico. She's with Nico. And if she could control Gaston…" He cast a desperate glance at Sander. "Can you maintain the bubble while you move?"

Sander grimaced. "I don't know. I think I'll have to drop it while I run, but I can re-initiate it once we're there."

"Then let's go." Bas strode for the door. He glanced back at Katalin, who hadn't moved. "You too, Kat. I don't know how far her reach is or whether she can maintain control over multiple people at once, but I'm taking no chances with any of you."

They all charged out of the room and along the corridor —Bas, Tarik, Sander, Katalin, and half a dozen guards. They thundered through the rotunda, passing a slack-jawed Ferran Rey and his cronies. Bas nearly stumbled to a stop, because there was no way Ferran couldn't know about his daughter's abilities. Hell, he'd probably been capitalizing on them to further his political agenda for years.

Later.

For now, Nico's safety was the only thing that mattered. The ice in Bas's middle had vanished, leaving fire in its wake.

As they barreled up the stairs and into the private wing, Genevieve wandered out from her quarters. Bas stumbled to a halt before he could run her down.

"Darling?" She blinked up at him, then beamed at Tarik. "And Tarik too! You didn't have to rush over so soon." She tilted her head, birdlike, as she took in the rest of the entourage. "And I don't think we need quite so many guards simply to discuss which color scheme you prefer."

"Color scheme?" Bas forced himself to remain calm, even though the hallway in front of his own quarters was empty of Pascal's hulking figure. "For what?"

"The wedding, of course. Ona's brought me all of Helena's selections, but she wants your input too."

Bas's belly dropped. "Ona." He looked past his mother's shoulder, and sure enough, Ona Rey was sitting at the tea table with what looked like a book of fabric swatches in her lap—and an extremely dumbfounded expression on her face. He turned to Sander. "Sander, if you could please engage your bubble here."

Sander bit his lip. "I'm not sure I can extend it all the way to your quarters."

"You don't have to."

Tarik grabbed Bas's arm. "Don't be an idiot, man. If she were to take control of you—"

"She hasn't managed to do it yet." He smiled wryly. "And I suspect she's been trying for years." He gripped Tarik's shoulder. "I'll be fine. But I want my mother protected." He gestured to the guards. "You lot, protect the Queen Consort. Keep the Duchess from leaving, but, Sander, keep her outside the bubble. Can you do that?"

Sander nodded and took up the position. Bas didn't feel any difference, but his mother put a hand to her forehead, wincing as if she had a massive hangover.

"Bastien? What's going on?"

He kissed her forehead. "Later, Mother. Stay here with the guards, and under no circumstances go anywhere near Ona Rey."

She sniffed, the sparkle back in her eyes. "As if I ever would. Why, do you know she had the nerve—"

Bas left her speaking indignantly to Katalin and raced down the hall. One set of footsteps pounded after him. He glanced over his shoulder. "Tarik, you've fallen victim to her before. Maybe you should hang back with your husband."

"Fuck no." He bared his teeth. "It's exactly because I've been a victim before that I'm your best wingman. I know what it's like, and I know what to look for in her fucking mental games. Now shut up and let's take this bitch down."

When Bas grabbed his sitting room doorknob and would have flung the door open, Tarik shook his head and indicated the bedroom door instead and mouthed *stealth approach.*

Bas nodded, hoping he'd remembered to disengage the deadbolt. *Nico.* He had to be all right. He *had* to be. What if Helena had taken over his mind and convinced him to leave? Or injure himself? Bas's heart felt as if it were beating outside his body. The sitting room balcony was directly over a wrought-iron fence tipped with three-pointed spear caps. If he'd fallen or jumped, he'd have been impaled even if the fall from third-story windows hadn't killed him first.

But as he and Tarik eased open the door and crept through the bedroom and into the dressing room, he could hear voices in the sitting room.

One of them was Helena's.

"—Rohypnol will do the trick."

"You can't seriously imagine you'll be able to control everybody in the country." *Nico.* Bas breathed a little easier. At least he was all right now and seemed to be not only in his right mind but aware of what Helena was.

"I don't have to control everybody. Political success is all about learning how to apply the appropriate pressure at the right inflection points. In fact, most people don't need to be controlled at all, at least not directly. Rumor, innuendo, flattery, the inclination of any disaffected group to give in to their mob tendencies. Convince them that their interests will be best served by a particular action, and they'll follow like sheep." She chuckled. "Of course, afterward they might not remember exactly why they decided to turn militant, but it hardly matters as long as the goal is achieved."

Red tinged Bas's vision. The protests. The insurrection. The attack that could have killed Nico. She was behind it?

"Your goal is treason, you know." Nico's voice wobbled a little.

Bas cursed, wishing he could see inside the room. Pascal must be in there. Was he restraining Nico? Holding a weapon on him? Bas didn't want to rush into the room only to make things worse.

"It's not treason!" Helena barked. "The traitors were the scum that sparked civil war, that instigated the Schism. But now, within my lifetime, that heinous wrong will finally be righted when, as Regent, I declare allegiance to the South Abarran crown and usher in a reunited Abarra. History will celebrate me as the person who ended centuries of wrongs. I'll be a heroine." Her throaty chuckle chilled Bas's blood, and if Tarik's shiver was any indication, it had the same effect on him. "I'll be a god."

Bas had had enough of this shit. He yanked open the door. "What you'll be is executed for treason, you conniving bitch."

Nico's belly swooped at the sight of Bastien standing in the doorway, practically breathing fire, with Tarik looming at his shoulder like an avenging angel's sidekick, both of them without a clue.

"Nico, don't move."

Bastien couldn't have timed his entrance more dramatically than if he were the star of the National Opera. But he didn't have all the facts. He didn't know what Helena had done, what she was capable of.

Or that she had a knife.

And at the worst possible time, a vision obscured Nico's sight.

Pascal hefting a marble side table and heaving it at Bastien at the same time that Helen launched her knife at him, Tarik looking on in horror.

He shook his head, willing the vision to fade so he could *see* again, because this foresight stuff was *bullshit. But what do I do?*

Was that what would happen if Nico did something? But what? What had he been thinking of before the vision hit? What question had he asked himself?

Not a question, but a statement. Two statements: Helena had a knife and Bastien had told him not to move. Ergo, if Nico complied with Bastien's request, it clearly would not turn out well.

So when Helena snapped her head around to sneer at Bastien, Nico didn't hesitate. He darted out from behind the chair and threw himself at her. He wasn't big and beefy like Pascal, but he was bigger than Helena and his weight would surely knock her off balance until Bastien and Tarik —both of them more versed in self-defense than Nico— could take over.

Unfortunately, Nico banged his shin on the tea table and lurched sideways, stumbling in an attempt not to faceplant at Helena's feet.

As he steadied himself, he caught the look of horror on Bastien's face as Helena, grinning as madly as the first Mrs. Rochester, lifted her knife and drove it down in a vicious arc, right at Nico's chest. Still off balance, Nico couldn't dodge, so braced himself for the blow, hoping that Helena's aim was worse with bladed weapons than it was with mind control.

"No!" Bastien shouted.

But an inch from Nico's sternum, it was as though the knife hit a barrier and slid to the side. Helena's momentum sent it down to tangle in her skirts.

She shrieked, a high, cringe-inducing sound as Tarik wrestled a reanimated Pascal and Bastien dodged the two of them to grab Helena's wrist.

"Drop the knife," he ground out between clenched teeth. "You've only yourself to blame if you stabbed yourself. I'd prefer to let you bleed to death, but it would ruin the carpet and I'd rather see you face trial and execution. Perhaps after a long, uncomfortable prison term."

But when Bastien lifted Helena's wrist, even though she continued to scream, the knife was blood-free. Was she shrieking out of fury or—

Oh!

Polita was attached to Helena's ankle with all four sets of claws, growling as she bit Helena's calf through her silk skirts.

Suddenly, the door burst open and Corin hustled in, followed by Katalin, Sander, the Minister of Powers, a pair of Ministry officers and, oddly enough, Queen Genevieve, who looked as if she wished for a knife of her own.

The Queen pointed to Helena. "There she is. Restrain her before she does even more damage to my family."

Apparently Helena couldn't mount any of her mind-control mojo with an angry kitten attached to her leg, because the Ministry officers were able to slap her into restraining irons without turning into zombies.

The instant they'd taken her into custody, Bastien practically leaped over the sofa and wrapped Nico in a tight embrace. "You're all right. You're not hurt. You're all right," he kept murmuring as if he were trying to reassure himself rather than Nico.

Nico allowed himself a moment to enjoy it—just a moment, because this whole bizarre interlude was about to come to a screeching halt. There was hardly any way that Parliament could insist Bastien marry a woman who not only wielded dangerous mind-control powers, but whose chief goal in life—other than being a god—was apparently to hand their country over to South Abarra.

But for now, he let himself hug Bastien back, because *he* was all right too. No longer in danger from someone who wished him irreparable harm.

Queen Genevieve drifted over and smiled at both of them, her eyes bright and clear. "Darling, is this your fiancé?"

Bastien exchanged a startled look with Nico before turning his gaze to the queen. "Yes, Mother. Are you—"

"Oh, stop it!" She batted his arm, probably with less force than Polita. "You needn't stare at me with that wild-eyed look, as if I'm the ghost of one of Louis's poor consorts. I'm fine." Her expression turned stormy. "Beastly Helena Rey. I *never* liked her as a match for you. That lovely Duke of Roses got Ona to admit that my...absent-mindedness was because I've been fighting Helena's coercive *suggestions* about your marriage." She *hmmph*ed. "And *Ona* is responsible for everyone thinking Helena was so beautiful all these years. That's her power. Cosmetic illusion." She turned to Nico. "Now *this* one doesn't need any enhancement, does he? He's so handsome!"

Nico flushed, but Bastien winked at him. "Yes. He is, isn't he? And brave. And smart. And heroic."

"I'm not heroic," Nico muttered. "All I did was stand here while she monologued at me."

Bastien pulled back and gripped Nico's shoulders. "Do you think I didn't miss the way you tried to tackle her?" He gave Nico a little shake. "We'll have to discuss that. I don't want you to put yourself in danger ever again."

Nico was about to reply that he'd hardly encounter this kind of excitement as a vineyard manager, but then he glanced around the room, which while spacious, was never intended to hold quite so many people, some of them larger than the average refrigerator.

Of course. Bastien still had to keep the pretense up. It would take a while for Lady Helena's crimes to be fully adjudicated, and with Parliament out of session, the contract was still in place. So he simply nodded, although he had to swallow several times to ease the tightness in his throat.

"When she attacked you with that knife, I thought my heart would stop." Bastien smoothed Nico's hair back. "In fact, if she'd succeeded, I'm pretty sure it would have."

Nico smiled, as the onlookers would undoubtedly expect. But Bastien didn't mean it. Not really. This was still an act for the benefit of their very interested audience—including his mother, for God's sake. He couldn't meet Bastien's eyes, so he glanced down at his own chest—miraculously not sporting a gaping hole, the smooth, green wool as pristine as Bastien's, his ceremonial sash unwrinkled.

Nico frowned, looking closer. Although the air was full of cat fur as Katalin detached Polita from Lady Helena with many words of praise, none of it besmirched his jacket, even though he'd held Polita against his chest earlier.

"Bastien, I didn't really evade her attack."

"Of course you did. She swung directly at you. She couldn't have missed."

"She didn't."

"She—" Bastien frowned, scanning Nico for nonexistent wounds. "Where are you hurt? Tarik! Call for a medic. We have to—"

"Calm down." Nico placed his hands on Bastien's chest, while he still had the right. "I mean, her blow glanced off me." He jerked his chin down at his uniform. "Just like cat fur apparently does too."

Bastien's eyebrows traveled halfway up his forehead. "You mean…"

"I mean, your deflection power doesn't just affect you. You can extend it to other people too."

Bastien blinked. "Are you sure?"

Nico shrugged. "Hard to argue with results."

"Hmmm." Bastien narrowed his eyes, then focused on the tea tray, miraculously still standing after Nico's close encounter with the table. He picked a scone, tossing it in his hand while a grin grew. Then he pivoted and threw it straight at Tarik.

It smacked him right in the chest, scattering crumbs all over his black blazer, before falling to the carpet at his feet. "What the *fuck*, Bas?" He blushed, glancing shamefacedly at Queen Genevieve. "Sorry, Auntie."

Bastien winked at Nico. "Apparently it doesn't extend to everyone."

Nico grasped Bastien's lapels. "Do me a favor and don't conduct any more tests."

Bastien gazed down at him, his eyes suddenly dark and intense. "I promise to behave if you promise me something in return."

Nico forbore rolling his eyes. "No, I won't put myself purposely in danger."

"That's not my request." Bastien gathered Nico into his arms again and murmured for his ears alone, "I know you signed on to be the king's ex, but would you consider a different title?"

The lump was back in Nico's throat again. *Does he want me to leave already? Leave the country?* "Like what?"

"Like King Consort."

Nico jerked, but Bastien stroked Nico's spine, petting him like he would Polita. "Bastien, that's not part of... We talked about this. You don't have to—"

"I know." Bastien raised his head and shot an apologetic glace at the others in the room. "If you all could give us a moment of privacy, please?"

Everyone trooped out, Queen Genevieve with a twinkling smile and Tarik with a knowing smirk. As soon as the door closed behind the last guard, Bastien dropped to one knee.

Nico sucked in a breath. "Bastien—"

"Nico. Will you please marry me for real? You don't have any obligation to say yes. In fact, I'd want you to say no unless you can answer me one thing truthfully."

Nico's throat was so thick he could barely speak. "What? he croaked.

"Do you love me?" Nico opened his mouth, but Bastien squeezed his hands. "Not as your king, but as a man. As a partner. As a husband. As someone who will stand by my side as we bring North Abarra into the twenty-first century. As we make it a place for *all* our people. Because I love you." He smiled wryly. "Rather desperately, as a matter of fact. Enough to let you go if you don't feel the same."

Nico's heart was lodged firmly in his throat. Once again, he tried to speak but only managed a strangled gasp.

Bastien kissed his palm. "I know the life of a Royal isn't what you wanted. It's a lot, as Tarik is fond of saying, usually with a vast array of expletives. There's an enormous amount of work ahead on behalf of our people and our county, work that can be tedious and frustrating and protocol-bound, even if you've been raised to it, as I was." Bastien rolled his eyes this time. "And the drama. Well, you've had an example today. So other than the fancy clothes and the excellent food and the superlative staff, there's not a lot to recommend it."

Nico swallowed, nudging his power to get off its ass. *If-this-then-that. Marry Bastien—yes or no?*

The *no* door rose before him. Behind it lay a neat little pied-à-terre, serene, sunny, well-appointed, yet somehow echoingly lonely, a single pair of shoes by the door.

He took a mental side-step and opened the *yes* door.

The palace gardens, Bastien beside him, Nico's hand in his. A little girl, perhaps three or four, was grubbing happily in the dirt in front of them.

"Papa! Aita! Look!" She grinned proudly, pointing as a pea shoot unfurled from the ground at her knees.

Aita. Basque for papa.

He took in a shaky breath as the vision faded. "You're wrong." He smiled down at Bastien. "This life does have something to recommend it."

Bas's expression turned painfully hopeful. "Really?"

"Of course. It has something I love more than anything in the world." Nico sank to his knees so he could take Bastien's face between his palms and press a chaste kiss to his lips. *A promise.* "It has you."

a message from

ej

Dear Reader,

Thank you so much for reading *King's Ex*, the third in my Royal Powers books. I'm so happy you've taken this journey with me! I'd be immensely grateful if you'd take a moment to leave a review at the retailer and any other site you use for reviews. Believe me, reviews make an *enormous* difference to the health and well-being of books (and not incidentally, to their associated authors!).

Wondering what to read next? If you're a fan of contemporary romance, you might like *Clickbait*, where love blossoms at a construction site, between a prickly web designer and a family-focused electrician. If you're in the mood for something a little less, er, reality-based, there's my Mythmatched story universe—paranormal romantic comedy, beginning with *Cutie and the Beast*, where a cursed fae warrior turned psychologist clashes with his determined temporary office manager. As you might expect, hi-jinks ensue!

Pop on over to my website, https://ejrussell.com, for all the deets on my books—my paranormal rom-coms and mysteries, my contemporary romances, and my one lone historical. If you're an audio fan, you can find the audio scoop there too. *King's Ex*, for instance, is narrated by the wonderful Kirt Graves. (The QR code below will get you there with your smartphone camera or other code reader.)

My newsletter is the place to get the latest dish on new releases, sales, and more. I promise I only send one out when I've got...well...news. You can subscribe here: https://ejrussell.com/newsletter.

All my best,
—E

Also by
ej

Paranormal Romance
Mythmatched Universe
Fae Out of Water Trilogy
Cutie and the Beast
The Druid Next Door
Bad Boy's Bard

Supernatural Selection Trilogy
Single White Incubus
Vampire With Benefits
Demon on the Down-Low

Other Mythmatched Romances
Howling on Hold
Possession in Session
Witch Under Wraps
Cursed is the Worst
The Skinny on Djinni
Assassin by Accident (part of Carnival of Mysteries)

Mythmatched Companion Stories
Rusty's Really Bad Day (free to newsletter subscribers)
Second First Date (free to newsletter subscribers)
First Flight (free to newsletter subscribers)

Quest Investigations Mysteries
Five Dead Herrings

The Hound of the Burgervilles
The Lady Under the Lake
Death on Denial

At Odds with the Gods (A Mythmatched / Purgatory
Playhouse crossover)

Art Medium Series
The Artist's Touch
Tested in Fire
Art Medium: The Complete Collection (omnibus edition)

Legend Tripping Series
Stumptown Spirits
Wolf's Clothing

Enchanted Occasions Series
Best Beast
Nudging Fate
Devouring Flame

Royal Powers Series (shared world)
Duking It Out
Duke the Hall
King's Ex

Magic Emporium Series (shared world)
Purgatory Playhouse

Monster Till Midnight

Science Fiction Romance
Sun, Moon, and Stars Series
Partnership
Principles

Historical Romance
Silent Sin

Contemporary Romance
Camera Shy
The Thomas Flair
Mystic Man
For a Good Time, Call... (A Bluewater Bay novel, with Anne
Tenino)

Christmas Kisses (holiday shorts)
The Probability of Mistletoe
An Everyday Hero
A Swants Soiree

Geeklandia Series
The Boyfriend Algorithm (M/F)
Clickbait

Writing as Nelle Heran
(traditional cozy mystery)

Crafty Sleuth Series (with C.K. Eastland)
Die Cut
Mixed Media
Found Objects (*coming soon*)

About the
Author

E.J. Russell (she/her), author of the award-winning Mythmatched paranormal romance series, writes LGBTQ+ romance and mystery in a rainbow of flavors. Count on high snark, low angst, and happy endings.

Reality? Eh, not so much.

She's married to Curmudgeonly Husband, a man who cares even less about sports than she does. Luckily, C.H. also loves to cook, or all three of their children (Lovely Daughter and Darling Sons A and B) would have survived on nothing but Cheerios, beef jerky, and Satsuma mandarins (the extent of E.J.'s culinary skill set).

E.J. also writes traditional cozy mystery as Nelle Heran. She lives in rural Oregon, enjoys visits from her wonderful adult children, and indulges in good books, red wine, and the occasional hyperbole.

News & Social Media:
Website: https://ejrussell.com
Newsletter: https://ejrussell.com/newsletter

Acknowledgements

A special thank you to Chris Cox for proposing the idea of a series about superpowered royalty, and to the other authors who have made playing in this sandbox such fun: Renae Kaye, Lynn Lorentz, Sara York, Jackie North, Liv Rancourt, Irene Preston, Louisa Baccio, and Mickey Quinn.

Thank you to Fern Lee for another adorable cover, Liv and Irene for beta reading, Meg DesCamp for editing and encouragement (aka browbeating), and Kcee Bomer for assistance and general good cheer.

Thanks to my family—Jim, Hana, Nick, Ross, and Billy—for not rolling their eyes when I say, "I've got a book releasing today!" Love you, guys!

And, always and forever, thank you to my readers for accompanying me on this journey. You're the reason I can continue to follow my heart, and I appreciate you more than I can say.